Another bride for a Branigan brother! You met Drew in *Bittersweet Harvest*—this is his brother Ryan's story.

For A Long Time Sky Stood Back,

watching Ryan and the group of kids work on her car.

Officer Branigan, who delivered babies and saved delinquents, had kissed her twice like there was no tomorrow. He made her hands clammy and her heart race just by raising his head from the depths of her car's engine and looking at her. She looked back, thoroughly enjoying the exchanges that were beginning to speak volumes.

Maybe she should ask him to dinner. Maybe he'd ask her to a movie. Maybe they could just walk over to his house and tear their clothes off. Maybe she should just go home.

Sky went back outside and raised her face to the bitter wind. Are we having fun? she asked the cranberry bogs. Dinner or a movie would be nice, a concert... Hell, she'd settle for a tour of the police station.

Dear Reader,

Welcome to Silhouette! Our goal is to give you hours of unbeatable reading pleasure, and we hope you'll enjoy each month's six new Silhouette Desires. These sensual, provocative love stories are both believable and compelling—sometimes they're poignant, sometimes humorous, but always enjoyable.

Indulge yourself. Experience all the passion and excitement of falling in love along with our heroine as she meets the irresistible man of her dreams and together they overcome all obstacles in the path to a happy ending.

If this is your first Desire, I hope it'll be the first of many. If you're already a Silhouette Desire reader, thanks for your support! Look for some of your favorite authors in the coming months: Stephanie James, Diana Palmer, Dixie Browning, Ann Major and Doreen Owens Malek, to name just a few.

Happy reading!

Isabel Swift
Senior Editor

LESLIE DAVIS GUCCIONE
Still Waters

Silhouette Desire

Published by Silhouette Books New York

America's Publisher of Contemporary Romance

With love for
Amy Sinnott Beers and
Harbormaster Donald C. Beers III,
and the members of their families, whose combined
knowledge of the criminal justice system,
police departments, emergency medical procedures,
fire fighting and municipal governments
has breathed life into my characters
and shaped my stories time and again.

SILHOUETTE BOOKS
300 East 42nd St., New York, N.Y. 10017

Copyright © 1986 by Leslie Davis Guccione

ISBN: 0-373-05353-3

First Silhouette Books printing May 1987
Second printing May 1987

America's Publisher of Contemporary Romance

Printed in the U.S.A.

LESLIE DAVIS GUCCIONE

says that she feels that the Branigans are part of her own family. Since writing *Bittersweet Harvest*, she has fallen in love with each of the Branigan brothers, and has enjoyed telling their stories.

Leslie lives with her husband and three children in a state of semichaos in a historic sea captains' district south of Boston. When she's not at her typewriter, she's actively researching everything from sailboats to cranberry bogs. What free time she has is spent sailing and restoring her circa 1827 Cape Cod cottage. Her ideas for her books are based on the world around her. As she states, "Romance is right under your nose." She has also written under the name Leslie Davis.

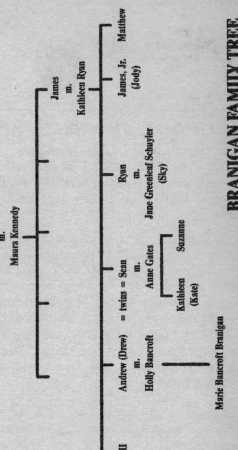

Kevin Branigan
m.
Maura Kennedy

Kevin, II   Andrew (Drew)   = twins = Sean   Ryan   James
                      m.   m.   m.   m.
              Holly Bancroft   Anne Gates   Jane Greenleaf Schuyler   Kathleen Ryan
                                                      (Sky)

                                Kathleen   Suzanne   James, Jr.   Matthew
                                 (Kate)   (Jody)

Marie Bancroft Branigan

BRANIGAN FAMILY TREE

One

Sky Cunningham smiled at the bittersweet memories as she ran her finger down the alphabetic listings in the Plymouth County telephone directory.

Branigan, Andrew & Holly B.
Branigan Cranberries, Inc.
Branigan, James, Jr., atty
Branigan, Kevin, P.
Branigan, Sean

No "Branigan, Ryan"... Amazing how much could be surmised from a phone book. Jane Greenleaf Schuyler Cunningham—Sky—took another belt of her coffee. Ryan could be living at the family house, which was Kevin's listing. Ryan could still be in the army and living anywhere Uncle Sam had sent him; Ryan could have taken up residence on the moon for all Sky knew. She was unaware of how heavily she sighed.

She looked back at the directory. Half of the six brothers had their own listing now. Drew had married; maybe they all had. In thirteen years anything could happen. She was a testament to that herself. James, or Jody as the family called him, was obviously practicing law in Plymouth, and the family business was booming. That bit of news had come not from the phone book, but *The Wall Street Journal*'s article on the cranberry industry. Branigan Cranberries of Millbrook, Massachusetts, was one of the largest of Ocean Spray's cooperative partners. She'd scanned the article for mention of Ryan, but only Kevin and Drew had been interviewed.

Sky drummed on the kitchen table with her fingers. What was it about finding yourself alone at thirty-one that made you question every past decision, every fork in the road? She shut the book, having learned one more thing. None of the phone numbers listed under "Branigan" coincided with the number in the Help Wanted column of the *Millbrook Ledger* where Bittersweet Bogs was advertising for seasonal pickers. Sky was relieved that she'd been hired by strangers.

Picking cranberries for a daily minimum wage—her father would turn over in his grave. Nevertheless, it was cash for a few days' work. It would keep her in groceries while she waited for the mounds of paperwork from Boston to unleash her from Mark's surname and for the trust fund to begin to flow so that she could make the refurbishing of Schuyler House a reality. The only thing cranberry picking required was a strong back and a pair of waders. Sky had told the woman who hired her over the phone that she had waders, and now, before she left for the bogs, she stuffed the *Ledger* into the toes of her brother's pair, abandoned for years in the mudroom of the old house.

Being five feet eight inches tall had its advantages. Her brother, Jake, was only five-ten, and with the exception of the boot size, the waders very nearly fit. When she'd finished getting ready, she put a log in the wood stove and left the house. Nights were brisk in October, but there was enough warmth from the autumn sun so that Sky had squeaked by heating only the kitchen. She slept upstairs in her unheated bedroom, leaving the rest of the cavernous rooms of the historic colonial house closed off. All of that was about to change.

She threw Jake's waders into the back of her thirteen-year-old Mercedes-Benz, eased the car from the carriage barn and headed through the village, which was alive with brilliant foliage. The bogs bordered the Millbrook Country Club on the Duxbury town line. When the woman had asked if she knew the spot, Sky had smiled into the receiver. Did she ever.

The last time she'd driven the route, Sky hadn't been prompt; she'd been late. The Mercedes had purred then, the way her heart had. The car had been a gift from her parents to commemorate her graduation from boarding school, her eighteenth birthday and upcoming debut. It hadn't been October then; it had been August, a clear hot night with the moon rising over the pines that bordered the dry cranberry acreage...

Ryan Branigan was already there, and her headlights washed the tailgate of his blue GMC pickup truck, neatly lettered with Branigan Cranberries on each door. A gold speck of light glowed as he took a final drag from his ever-present cigarette and ground it out beneath his heel. Sky caught the quick whiff of breath freshener he sprayed into his mouth before tucking the little canister into his jeans. She turned off her ignition.

Work boots were the style, and his were crossed at the ankles. Ryan leaned back against the truck, denim from jacket to jeans, the picture of confidence. The ratty red bandanna, which was his trademark, held back his shaggy black hair. Sky thought then that he looked even more perfect than he did during the day when he rode the club's tractor, manicuring the grounds, more often than not, naked to the waist.

"Thought you weren't comin'," he said.

She gave him the devilish grin she was famous for and savored a sense of risk that made her shiver. "I couldn't just push my chair back from the Feltons' dinner table and scram, you know. They even made me a cake with Bon Voyage on it. Susan's going to cover if my folks call."

Adolescent awkwardness lay just beneath the bravado in both of them. They didn't touch. His eyes moved from her kid-leather sandals to the trim fit of her summer frock. "You're all dressed up."

"Not really. It was a present from Gram in Palm Beach. Mom made me wear it."

"Too bad it's not one of your little tennis dresses." Ryan was warming up.

So was she. With a poke to his chest, she smiled back. "I saw you this afternoon, pretending to weed the hedge next to the courts. You're lucky you made it through the summer without getting canned for lurking in the bushes."

They were quiet again, and the air was pregnant with everything they'd left unsaid since the end of June. Sky couldn't have cared less about tennis, but on her first Saturday home from school, there'd been a coming-out party at the club. Ryan's first Saturday on the job had entailed parking the cars. It had seemed to be the most painfully romantic moment of her life when their eyes locked over the open door of her brand-new car and even more so when she'd discovered—after considerable snooping—that the eighteen-year-old employee was one of "the" Branigan brothers.

Ryan was the fourth of six orphaned brothers, who were being raised by Peter Bancroft, a bachelor neighbor. He not only acted as guardian, but also managed their legacy—the cranberry bogs. To say that Sky and Ryan's paths might not have crossed otherwise was putting it mildly. Millbrook and the cranberry crop that sustained the third generation Boston Irish brothers were hearth and home to them.

Schuyler House, on the edge of the village common, in Millbrook's historic district, was a quirky white elephant Sky's mother tolerated to appease her husband's family. Sky and her brother lived there briefly each summer between school and camp. "Real life" was spent in Palm Beach or the Greenleaf Mansion on Beacon Hill. An extraordinary-looking child since birth, Jane Schuyler grew into a blue-eyed, blond-haired vision with the confidence to carry her height gracefully like the thoroughbred she was. What social gulf lay between Sky and the object of her mad crush was bridged by the physical perfection of the match though Sky's nature was to ignore conventions, anyway.

Like his brothers, Ryan had reached a height of six feet by his seventeenth birthday. He had the Black Irish, Branigan green eyes under dark hair and an unfreckled complexion given to deep flushes that Sky found irresistible. His body was firm and muscular from the rigorous physical demands of his family's business. He went as far as any girl would let him, and Janey Schuyler made his blood boil just by lowering her lashes.

Sky handled her crush the way she handled everything she did—open throttle, full steam ahead. She had ten different ways of saying "I dare you" without opening her mouth, which exhausted her parents and incited her suitors. Ryan Branigan's green gaze was the only one that dared her back.

If a silver-gray Mercedes were as much a thrill to him as the girl who drove it, that was okay, too. Sky, if she'd ever stopped to analyze it, would have had to admit that her parents' disapproval added to Ryan's appeal, the same way her car did to hers.

Since he was employed at the club full-time for the summer, Sky had taken up tennis with a vengeance, and when she hadn't been on the courts, she'd lounged around the pool. Her parents had caught on shortly after Ryan had and handled the situation with typical Schuyler restraint. They had fretted when other invitations were put aside, held their tongues when she had him escort her to her season's debutante parties, but they neither encouraged nor discouraged the relationship. It had been their fondest prayer that the romance would burn itself out by Labor Day, when she'd leave for college in Virginia.

However, the first Friday in August, Ryan's twenty-four-year-old brother Kevin had deposited a notably inebriated Sky at her father's granite doorstep. John Schuyler had been told Ryan was "not well" and had been left in the care of his twin brothers Drew and Sean. That had been all the details the senior Schuylers ever got.

Sky had protested with typical bravado that she was within two weeks of the legal drinking age, and they should have been glad it was just beer, anyway. She'd slept it off and awoke to the news that her final weeks of summer would be spent on a musical tour of Austria.

Now, on the eve of her departure, she and Ryan were quiet. Ryan looked out over the golf course, and his classic features looked pinched. Summer color, heightened by the moment, washed his cheeks. One of Sky's favorite pastimes, besides challenging his aggressive behavior, was guessing at the emotions he rarely admitted to. "Miss me?"

He nodded and put his arm around her sweatered shoulder, letting his fingers brush the fullness at the edge of her breast. Sometimes she swatted him away, sometimes she didn't. Right now she was so full of exquisite sadness, that she stepped into a hug. She pressed herself against his chest so she could feel his sigh and hoped he was as sad as she.

"Some summer, huh?" he said against her cheek in a thick voice.

She nodded. "Millbrook Country Club never had such a weed-free set of tennis courts." She let his arm tighten, and they were still again. She could have stayed like that for hours, but the more she hugged him back, the closer she came to tears. When she pushed him away, she took both his hands. "So I guess you get to be the boy I left behind."

His green eyes glistened. "I guess so."

She tried a smile. "Let's not be too sad. I'll have a few days at home between Europe and college."

He nodded, and when he tried to move his hands, Sky opened his fingers and pressed them to her heart as fat tears began their slow descent over her cheeks. She wasn't in love with Ryan, of course. She had spent the better part of the summer telling herself that. There was enough blue blood and common sense in her to convince her that what she was feeling was what Ryan's brothers called "hormone overdrive."

The night Kevin and the twins had come home and caught them in the Branigan living room, she'd been lectured all the way home about physical attraction and alcohol and slowing down. That's what she loved about Ryan, however—the way he raced through life. He had the family business waiting for him, and till he was ready for that, he did what others dreamed of, and that included dating Jane Greenleaf Schuyler. The social gulf between them and educational differences weren't discussed; there was no point. The world lay in front of them, and Sky knew that for her it meant lots of boys as handsome and fun as Ryan, but with credentials and polish to match. She just wished everything inside her didn't ache so much at the thought of giving him up.

Ryan pressed his fingers over her dress. She was within days of menstruating, and her breasts were tender, but his touch made her feel alive. Her hair had been frosted that summer, and he caught it with his free hand and let the moonlight play in it. "You always smell so good," Ryan whispered, and she laughed. "Really. Your perfume stays on my shirts a little. Sometimes I sleep in them."

His smile was suddenly shy, and she nearly melted into the grass. She brushed his temple and played with the knot of his bandanna as he tilted his face against her hand. She kissed him, and he kissed her back. They kissed and sighed and kissed some more until their knees were weak, and they sank against each other to the earth. She knew every move he would make. Sometimes Ryan waited for encouragement and sometimes he didn't. The minilength shift moved up her thigh where his hand brushed her skin. He was encouraged. The August air was full of peepers, the distant croak of a bullfrog in the pond that fed the bogs and the muffled sighs of two sweethearts saying goodbye.

Disheveled but clothed, they clung to each other, moving steadily in one direction until Ryan rolled over and swore into the grass he'd spent all summer grooming. "Hormone overdrive," Sky gasped, and as he pressed himself against the ground Sky looked from the stars back to her teenage dream. She slipped his wallet from his hip pocket and rustled through it until she found the hermetically sealed packet he was never without. When he raised his head, she waved it under his nose. "Branigan," she whispered, "you've been dangling this at me all summer. We might as well use it."

"Dynamite!" he shouted, and when she clamped her palm over his mouth, he kissed it and mumbled it again.

Much later they walked along the edge of the golf course and through the stand of pines that bordered the bogs. His quiet nature was deep as a well, unfathomable. The air was electric with the tension until they reached the truck and he pulled her to him, and whispered, "Have a great time in Austria."

That was it? "Right. Seven other girls and me, two chaperones and a bunch of dead guys' music. We even have to go to the opera." Why were they talking about Europe! she wondered.

"Opera's not so bad...some of it. Peter plays it around the house a lot. It's okay," Ryan replied.

Had *she* been okay? Didn't he know it had been her first time and she needed to hear something, anything?

"I guess you'll have something to think about when you sit through those recitals. I'll never cut that grass again," he said with a laugh.

She punched him playfully as a trickle of relief replaced her anxiety. She'd never felt shy around him or so out of control. It was kind of scary and delicious at the same time. "So you'll think about it, too?"

His eyes shone in the shadowed light. "I'll never forget it."

"Branigan?"

"Hmm?"

"How about once more just to make sure you'll remember?" She laughed as his eyes widened. If any heart were to break, let it be tomorrow when passion no longer carried them.

"Damn it, Sky, I don't have another—"

She pressed her fingertips over his mouth and cocked her head. "My period's due any day. It's safe."

He looked beyond her to the Mercedes and back to his truck. "Your place or mine?"

"Definitely yours," she said, and they climbed into the cab. Sky had expected ecstasy, not a searing sadness that tore her heart out. She wanted to lie down with him forever, her mind a blank, her body singing. Ryan knew as well as she that this was all there was, all there would ever be, and never had words seemed less important. This time she held him and touched him and made him slow down so she'd never forget.

"Oh, God," he whispered, "Janey Schuyler..." The despair in his voice was the only hint that more than one heart was breaking.

She was in Lisbon by the next afternoon and Paris the day after that. She and seven others who were so much like her did the Louvre before they left for Vienna. In her pocketbook, Sky carried Ryan's bandanna, her wallet, passport and a half a dozen tampons. She had yet to need them. She arrived in Austria and would have given anything for the cramps she usually hated. With every trip—and they were painful—to the public rest rooms, her anxiety worsened.

The tour was led by Louise Forbes of the Wellesley College music department who happened to have been Sarah Schuyler's college roommate. The conspiracy wasn't as bad as Sky had feared. The other girls were all from the greater Boston area, slightly older than she and equally as rich. They were also willing to raise hell when the occasion warranted, and Sky wished like anything that she'd just get her period so she could relax and enjoy herself.

She missed Ryan terribly, but she was a realist above all. The college men her companions talked about seemed the height of maturity, and when the girls discovered she was going off to Hadley, they gave her the names of Southern families to look up, from Charlottesville to Chapel Hill. Her roommate for the tour was a nineteen-year-old named Amy Baker who asked about the significance of the bandanna.

"Great-looking townie I fooled around with in Millbrook," Sky told her nonchalantly. It was the only time she mentioned Ryan. The trip did much for her musical education and even more for her anticipation of college. By the middle of the second week, she could tell Beethoven from Haydn and Mozart, and knew the four best eating clubs at Princeton.

On the morning of her eighteenth birthday, with three days left on the tour, she threw up. She was queasy the minute she opened her eyes and laid under the down-filled duvet with her fist against her stomach, telling herself it was nerves, praying it was nerves. It was a little late for prayer, but she gave it her best shot. The nausea hit full force when she tried to brush her teeth, and she swayed at the sink, balling handfuls of her calico nightgown in her fists. It was soaked with perspiration by the time she turned on the shower. She held her breath until she could cry under the steamy spray and damned herself, Ryan, the country club, mother nature and hormones. She was still clammy with fear when she dressed. If her moments with Ryan had been the summer's brightest, these were the darkest.

The walking tour of Vienna did little to take her mind off anything. The smell of sauerbraten along the Ringstrasse turned her inside out, and she sat through a Bach organ recital at St. Stephen's without hearing a note. After dinner Mrs. Forbes insisted that Sky accompany her to the gift shop for a Brueghel print she knew her mother would love, and after twenty minutes of small talk, Sky finally escaped to the elevators.

Seven female voices shouting "Surprise!" and "Happy Birthday!" as she entered her room shattered what was left of her composure, but she tried to let them all know the tears were from joy. There were gifts and Sacher torte and lots of champagne.

"Here's to Sky and Sigma Chi," someone chanted.

"Deke, Saint A and Chi Phi..."

"Princeton, Dartmouth, Chapel Hill..."

"And don't forget to take your pill!"

She looked bleakly at Amy. "I shouldn't be drinking."

"You're eighteen, Sky; it's even legal at home!" her friend replied as she handed her the glass. "You're eighteen, and you're in Vienna!"

"I'm eighteen and I'm pregnant." The statement brought the revelry to a screeching halt. Seven faces looked at her sympathetically, but no one spoke for a long, painful moment. Then they all did.

Hours later in the dark, Sky rolled over and looked at the next bed. "Amy?"

"Yes," she replied sleepily.

"Thanks. I probably shouldn't have told anybody, but I feel much better."

"That's what friends are for, Sky."

She was woozy again in the morning and clung to the assurance from Amy that it was champagne or nerves. They were to head home by way of Rome, and Sky used the rest room in the hotel lobby as they checked out. She used the women's lounge in the Vienna airport, and hours later, while Mrs. Forbes dealt with Italian customs and passports, she left the band and went in search of *il gabinetti*. Moments later, brushing aside tourists and tears, she addressed the expectant members of her little band. "Anybody got a tampon?"

Two

The group parted at Logan airport in Boston with frantic promises of a Christmas reunion, hurried introductions to one another's parents and quick, meaningful squeezes for Sky. She collapsed into the back seat of her parents' Lincoln and listened to her mother's idle chitchat as they worked their way south to the Plymouth exit.

"You're awfully quiet, Jane," Sarah said.

"Jet lag. It was a great trip, really." Sky talked briefly about the tour, then dozed till they got to Millbrook. The first of her three days at home was spent unpacking and repacking footlockers and luggage for college. She thought a lot but didn't do a thing about what was on her mind. The second day Amy called from Pride's Crossing on the north shore to wish her well. She urged her to see Ryan.

"He hasn't called *me*, you know," Sky said.

"Does he even know you're home?"

"He knew my schedule. Besides, things would never be the same.... I could never tell him. It was my fault to begin with, and if we got together, he'd just expect to do it again. He's probably done it about a million times." She sighed heavily and wished Amy were right there in the room, just as she'd been in Europe. "After we—you know—did *it*, he didn't even say anything. I know he thinks I'm a spoiled brat with no experience. Telling him about everything would just be icing on the cake."

"Experience? Sky, you're barely eighteen; how much experience are you supposed to have?"

"Oh, Amy, enough to know how to protect myself and act like a woman. I'm never letting anybody near me again until I know what I'm doing. It's not like we were in love or anything." She wondered if she sounded convincing. "You can bet he's over me by now. He can have any girl in Millbrook. It was a great summer, but that's all it was."

They hung up with more promises to keep in touch. On Sky's last free afternoon, she drove to the club for a swim, taking the Duxbury Road, past the bogs. She barely turned her head. She avoided glancing at the tennis courts or the golf course and headed right for the entrance and the pool's parking area.

She came out of the bathing house in her bikini and dove cleanly into the deep end, swimming the length of the pool with sure, even strokes. At the tile steps she watched two young mothers holding their toddlers, then dipped her head, slicking her long hair back. She pulled herself out with a shower of spray and found Ryan Branigan sitting on a beach towel directly in front of her.

Sky realized how shocked she must have looked when he blushed. He got to his feet as she stood on the cement trying not to stare at his wet cutoffs and new blue bandanna. Droplets of water clung to his chest, and it would be nearly Halloween before the image of his green eyes and guarded expression would fade from her memory.

"Hi," he said, shoving his hands into his pockets.

"Hi," Sky replied, wishing she had some place to put hers.

"Thought you left for Virginia today." He shifted his weight from one bare foot to the other.

"Tomorrow."

He nodded. "Well, good luck and everything. I hope school goes well. How was Europe? Did you like those dead guys' operas after all?"

She smiled. "Yeah, I guess I did. Beethoven's not so bad."

His clear, dreamy stare floated over her, but there weren't any flip remarks. Instead he met her eyes. "I thought you might send a card or something."

Sky's heart hammered. "I was awfully busy, moved around a lot."

"Sure. What the hell. Send me one from Hadley. You'll be back for Thanksgiving?"

Sky shook her head. "We'll be in Boston. I've got lots of coming-out stuff, boring parties, you know. Millbrook's a drag for my mother, anyway. We're just here summers." This was goodbye talk, and she hated it. She hated her nervousness, and she hated him for just standing there looking back at her. Boy, had she learned a lesson. She touched the bandanna, and the way his eyes closed made her heart hurt. "Well, tell all those brothers of yours I said goodbye, and Mr. Bancroft, too. See you next summer maybe."

"Right," Ryan said.

Without looking back, Sky turned and dove from the shallow end into the pool. She heard the lifeguard's whistle and knew it was for her, but she didn't stop until she was back by the diving board. "That was a stupid thing to do, Sky," the guard said.

She apologized, then added, "I thought employees weren't supposed to use club facilities."

The guard looked back in the direction from which she'd come. "Ryan Branigan? He quit two weeks ago. He's been hanging out here as a guest with Diana Middleton for the past few days. Past few nights, too," he cracked.

Sky dripped her way back into the lockers. She changed into shorts, put her hair in a ponytail and left for the parking lot. Ryan, who had pulled on a polo shirt to meet club regulations, was leaning against her Mercedes. He was blushing. "Sky," he said when she'd arrived, "Everything's—you know—all right?"

"'All right'?"

"Sky..." He looked miserable.

"What?" Then it dawned on her. No, everything wasn't all right. Everything was horribly confused, her insides, her outsides, feelings she didn't know she had and feelings she was afraid of having.

"Hell," he mumbled at his feet, and she laughed. Mr. Cool Guy had lost his mother at twelve, never had any sisters and was probably too self-conscious to ask Peter Bancroft the first thing about the workings of womens' bodies and "that stuff."

"Are you asking if I'm pregnant?" She laughed out of nervousness, but it sounded confident.

"Forget it, Sky. I just thought I should say something, okay?"

She gave him the lie of the century. "Thanks, but it's no big deal." She reached for her door handle and knew instantly that he thought she was reaching for him. He touched her face with one hand and the wet rope of her hair with the other. She recoiled against the front fender in some instinctive attempt to keep her feelings at bay.

He shoved his hands back into wet pockets. "I get the hint," he said, and then, as if it had been staged, another bikini-clad figure in an impatient pose called from the chain-link fencing edging the pool.

They both looked at her and then back at each other. Sky yanked open the door of the Mercedes; Ryan touched her arm. His parting words were called from a currently popular song. "If you can't be with the one you love..." It was bravado the likes of which only two eighteen-year-olds could pull off.

Sky gave up dreams of Ryan for fraternity men and perfected the habit of dating until chastity became an issue. She substituted the fine art of flirting for passion and kept half a dozen guys on a string. She acquired a taste for wine, philosophy and homecoming crowns at three campuses in three years.

She spent Thanksgiving and Christmas in the Greenleaf mansion on Beacon Hill in order to enjoy her debutante season and gave a rousing house party in Palm Beach for New Year's Eve. In February of that first year, she received a postcard of an aerial view of the barracks of Fort Ord, California, sent in care of the college. It read: *Roses are red, violets are blue, they took my bandanna and I miss you.* There was a valentine heart, with no return address and *This sure isn't Vienna* on the back. Sky pinned it on her bulletin board with the gift cards she'd received for the five flower arrangements that filled the room. John Schuyler, senior, died in April, shaking the family and giving Sarah the excuse to leave Schuyler House in the hands of Millbrook Realtors, rented out as an investment and retained on the off chance that some family member might want it someday....

The thirteen years' distance made most of the memories pleasant, the sorrows chalked up to youth and naïveté. Sky laughed now as she pulled her old car off the road and onto the sandy shoulder next to the bogs. Being back in Millbrook was dredging up memories faster than she could keep them down. She looked at the neighboring golf course where two diehards in parkas were pulling their own carts.

The bogs were divided down the middle by a raised dike, wide enough to be used as a cart path for trucks and the water reels needed for the harvest. The bog on the left was crimson with floating berries. To the right a figure stood on the reel as the machine's beater rotation churned up the crop. The foliage was brilliant, the sky blue and clear. It was her first fall in the little town, and it was beautiful. As she watched the harvest, a battered station wagon and a new truck pulled in next to her Mercedes.

Two men got out of the station wagon and, without waiting, pulled on waders. They walked toward a distant flatbed truck with wooden rails for sides, parked to catch cranberries as they were pulled up along a conveyor belt from the bog and dropped. Sky was mildly surprised to see a woman slide from the truck beside her—a sandy-haired blonde about her own age, who, at closer range, looked pregnant. They shook hands.

"Jane Cunningham? I'm Holly Branigan. I talked with you on the phone."

Sky's immediate response was to turn and look at the three men on the bogs and then back. "Branigan? I thought... These are Branigan bogs? The ad said Bittersweet.'' She'd even cross-checked the telephone numbers.

"Bittersweet is the Bancroft part of the business. I inherited it from Peter Bancroft and bought these this summer. My husband Drew and I run them along with the bogs his brothers own.''

His brothers; Sky didn't ask which they might be. So this was the wife of one of the twins. She smiled as Holly continued.

"This is the first year we've had to hire out. We got bigger and so did I.'' Holly laughed and patted her stomach. "Anyway, if you're a local then I'm sure you know as much about harvesting as I do. It's only my second season.'' She pointed to the men who'd arrived in the station wagon. "The Mendes brothers are old hands, too. Let them handle the loading. The engine running the conveyor belt is very temperamental. Drew and his brother got into a terrible fight over me last year on that thing. The truck rails collapsed and they both wound up in the hospital.'' She laughed. "It's a long story, but I'm supervising over here 'cause we're short handed and I want to prove to them that I can handle more than the books without major disaster!'' She looked at the waders Sky had pulled from her car. "Are you sure those things fit you?''

Sky nodded. "I adjusted them before I came. They'll be fine; don't worry about me.''

Holly looked as though she might, nevertheless. She walked Sky to her partners who broke from their Cape Verdian Portuguese to put her to work. Holly left, and Jorge, a weathered professional in his fifties, showed Sky how to open the hinged strips of wood that made up a bog-sized corral, and use it to push the berries toward the belt. As Jorge and his brother Juan watched, Sky got into her waders. With the shoulder straps hitched all the way up, the bib front gaped but covered her breasts. She looked like a clown in need of stuffing and was, no doubt, the only migrant worker in Millbrook whose work shirts and thick fisherman-knit sweater had Neiman Marcus labels.

"You sure, miss?" Juan asked.

"Absolutely." She moved cautiously into the shin-deep water and found that if she slid her feet over the rough bottom of the bog and didn't try to lift her feet too much she kept her balance on the submerged, bushy plants. With the roar of the reel across the dike and that of the belt at the truck, she was left to her task and her thoughts.

The tiny marble-size berries rode the conveyor belt and tumbled dripping into the confines of the truck, leaving small mounds of soaking hulls under the mechanism. Sky worked and thought about the two Branigans up there arguing about Holly. Maybe both twins were in love with her. Holly looked to be about Sky's age. Maybe Ryan had fallen in love with her, too. Maybe Ryan was right in town, harvesting the bogs at his house, doing just what she was with rakes and belts and lumbering trucks.

Sky worked diligently through the day, stopping for lunch and picking up again with the Mendes at two. The air was chilly and the water sparkling as the sun headed for the tops of the pines. At about three the red truck returned, and Holly got out with a clipboard on her hip. Even in her maternity clothes and man-sized jacket, she looked efficient and businesslike. While she stood at the far edge of the bog, a squad car pulled off the road and rambled up next to the Branigan truck. Sky's heart jolted as a uniformed officer got out and talked to Holly. Sky was squinting behind the corral in the middle of the bog.

He had on blues and a black leather jacket with the gold smudge of a seal at the shoulder. His black boots rose to his knees, as if he rode horses. The car had the town seal and Millbrook Police on the door—a local cop. Bad news? Another accident at the bogs? A blue uniform didn't automatically mean disaster. Sky kept pushing the berries with her long-handled wooden rake, watching from the corner of her eye. Their body language didn't indicate any emergency. The officer walked to her old Mercedes, and Sky gulped as Holly pointed to her.

Oh, God. Her heart stopped. Her mother was dead in Palm Beach. Her brother Jake and his family had gone down in a plane...the wood stove! Schuyler House was in flames. The officer began to walk along the edge of the bogs. She looked at the Mendeses; maybe they were illegal aliens. It couldn't be her, nobody knew she was here. That's when she stumbled. Her newspaper-padded toe caught the edge of the underwater sprinkler system, which at first she didn't feel. She went down on one knee and pitched forward to avoid impaling herself on the rake handle. It was an oafish slow-motion gesture that caught the bib at its widest gap. Before she could get up, she filled up like a water balloon, gallons of the icy stuff sluicing over every inch of her inside the waders.

Had she been in a pond, as happens with duck hunters, she would have drowned like a gangster sunk in cement. Here, in less than three feet of water, she floundered to the edge of the bog like a beached whale, soggy, dangerously chilled and thinking that she wasn't doing a damn thing for Holly's reputation.

The officer had been sauntering over, but he broke into a run and reached her as she sat up. He came down on one knee as she looked up into his face.

"My God, it is you. Janey Schuyler's back in town."

"Ryan!" She blinked at the low sunlight as she began to shake. Her teeth chattered.

Without asking, he clasped her roughly under the arms and got her farther onto her feet, yanking the suspender from her soaking shoulders. She helped with numb fingers as he stripped the heavy waterproof contraption off her sopping clothes. Although his expression was concerned, he was making an effort not to laugh. Steam rose from her as she shook.

He fingered the misshapen sweater. "Wool?"

"Acrylic," she chattered. "Ryan, you're a cop!"

He was already pulling the sweater over her head. "I know. Take this off; it'll make you colder. Come on." With an arm around her, he walked toward the squad car. She held the waders at arm's length and dropped them onto the hood of her car. Ryan had the sweater, all the while keeping her tight against his leather jacket. She could feel the pistol and holster against her hip as they hurried.

At the patrol car, he opened the trunk and took out a neatly folded blanket that he wrapped around her shivering frame. The first boy she had ever loved had her rolled in a blanket and was rubbing her down like a racehorse. He stared into her blue eyes as if he still couldn't believe whom he was rescuing.

"Get in the squad car," he said. "You've got to get home and into a shower."

Holly, who'd hurried the others back to work, approached with her jacket off and her mouth agape. "Jane, are you all right?"

Sky nodded. "I'm sorry."

Ryan refused Holly's offer of the outerwear. "I'll keep her in a blanket. She'll be fine."

Holly looked at her brother-in-law. "Jane Cunningham is *Sky*?"

The officer gave her a quick, uncomfortable nod and opened the passenger door.

Holly patted Sky's blanket. "Listen to him: he's an emergency medical technician. Go get rid of the chill. I'll drive your car home when we've quit for the day."

"Thanks," Sky replied.

"I assume you're in the white colonial on Main street, on the other side of the common from the fire station."

Sky looked at Ryan, who was pointing his index finger at Holly and already putting the car into gear. "Don't you have work to do?" His sister-in-law laughed and turned from the car.

Sky's bones ached with the chill as she huddled under the damp scratchy blanket. She sneaked a look at Ryan as he maneuvered the patrol car from the sandy spot back onto the road. *Gorgeous as ever.* He turned suddenly to look at her as she dropped her gaze to the Millbrook Police Department patch on his shoulder. Of all people...

She was the first to speak. "I gather you've mentioned me to Holly."

A smile played at his mouth. "Once or twice." Over the cackle of the police radio, he called in everything that had just happened. "Thirty-one-year-old female," he was saying. "I'm taking her home." When the mike was back in its spot, he added, "She reminds me of you sometimes. I guess I've mentioned it."

"Once or twice," Sky said.

This time Ryan's smile was broad. The car entered the village limits and passed the fire station. On the east side of the common a mix of imposing houses, wood-framed shops and white clapboard churches faced the residential row across the grassy park. The historic district began where Pilgrim Street bisected Main and ended beyond Schuyler House where a small Greek Revival house now served as headquarters for the Historical Commission. Every building constructed before 1860 had a small plaque to the left of the front door with its date and builder. The one on Sky's house read: Captain Joshua Schuyler, 1832.

"So you're back in town," Ryan said when he'd pulled into her driveway.

"So are you," she chattered, gripping the blanket.

"I have been for a while, five years, I guess. Your father been renting this out?"

Sky nodded. "Mother, actually. My father died when I was in college. I'm back to see about renovations and taking up residence again. Dad left a trust for the maintenance to Schuylers over thirty. I'm sure he thought he'd live to see us all well beyond that age, but he didn't, and since my mother had no interest, we rented it." She was shaking in earnest, and Ryan cut short the conversation.

"You're risking hypothermia. Let's get you into the house."

"What's the remedy?" Sky asked as she fumbled with the lock on the door to the mudroom.

He smiled again. "In severe cases we recommend taking your clothes off—body heat works wonders." For an opening conversation after thirteen years, it wasn't bad, and they both laughed. "This car patrols that stretch routinely but we don't get much call for the blanket till kids fall through the ice."

She led him into the kitchen. "Ever catch any parkers out there by the golf course?" She hoped he might blush.

He didn't. "Let's get you warmed up."

Sky huddled at the wood stove while Ryan peeled off the blanket and her socks. When she was barefoot, he used the phone to call in a Signal Five to let the station know he'd left the car. She warmed her hands and fluffed her curls.

"You cut your hair," he said lightly when he'd hung up.

"So did you," she responded, letting her gaze linger a fraction longer than he seemed comfortable with.

Ryan cleared his throat. "Well, you better get yourself into a warm shower. Any family here?"

Sky shook her head. "I'll be fine. Jake's coming Friday night. We're going to take room measurements, get stuff ready for the restoration. I hope to restore it after the first of the year, get some of the character back into it. It'll keep me off the streets."

"The character *is* back in it, I'd say."

She shook her head at him. "I won't move permanently till after Christmas, if that's what you meant. Anyway, thanks for the ride. I'll be fine as soon as I get that shower."

He shifted his weight. "See that you do. Not hot, a warm soak, and no liquor or caffeine for a few hours, either."

"I promise," she answered. "Really, I'll be fine."

"I know. I'd just feel better if somebody—Jake—were here. If you need anything, call Holly." As he spoke, he pushed back his jacket. Sky watched his hand skim over the pistol as he pulled his wallet from his hip pocket. He flipped it open in front of her, and then, as if the memory of how often he'd pressed her that summer sprang into his head, he stopped. "Hell," he mumbled.

Sky was the first to laugh. "Still carry them, Branigan?"

Ryan looked startled, and then he laughed, too. "I guess there's no use pretending I don't remember."

"Guess not," she said.

He found what he was looking for and handed her a Bittersweet Bogs business card. "Holly's number. They can always reach her on the CB, too. I mean it, call if you need anything before Friday."

Sky took it and caught sight of a wallet-sized photo of a redhead with two little girls. Baby Branigans. Well, why not, she thought. Her flirtatious mood dimmed, and she realized how miserably cold she was. "Thanks for your concern, but I'm all grown up. I can take care of myself."

His green eyes, clear as cat's eye marbles, shocking under the thick black hair, came back to hers. "Sky, you always could."

Three

She went upstairs as Ryan left the house and stood in the shower till the hot water ran out. It chased the chill, but nothing less than icy spray would have doused the sensations dancing over her. Certainly she'd thought about him over the years but it had been in a curious, nostalgic sort of way. She'd been totally unprepared for the depth of her physical response. She smiled as she dressed. Some attractive woman had obviously taken him out of the running, someone probably far more appropriate than Sky ever was. Well, good for them, she thought. Still, it was fun feeling eighteen again.

At five-thirty, with her hair fluffed dry, she was back in the kitchen in cords, molding a meat loaf. She found a fuzzy, "Bradenburg Concerto" on a Cape Cod radio station, which she was humming along with as the Mercedes' headlights washed the side of the house as it was driven up to the carriage barn. There was a quick rap on the mudroom door.

"Come in, Holly," she yelled as she washed her hands. "I'm so sorry I made such a mess this afternoon. I hope I haven't ruined your reputation with those gorgeous Branigan—" She turned from the sink in the middle of her quip and gave a little gasp. "Well, if it isn't one of the gorgeous Branigans himself," she mumbled as she caught sight of Ryan. Sky was nothing if not quick on her feet. He looked as though he remembered that, too.

"Holly's still tied up, and I'm off duty and was in the neighborhood." He was in a heavy crew-neck sweater, jeans and work boots.

"Now you look like the Branigan I remember," she added, feeling the need to restrain herself from letting her eye wander. "Where are your cigarettes?"

"Quit in the army."

"Good for you," she said, feeling the need to busy her hands with the dish towel. "Since Holly isn't here, will you apologize for me? I'm not usually so clumsy—who can forget my agility on the tennis courts?" There was a hint of surprise when she looked back at him. "I suppose I'm fired."

"Hardly. Holly sent over a pair of her own waders and the message that she'll see you at nine—same bogs. The job is yours for the rest of the week."

"No kidding," Sky replied.

"Would an officer of the law lie?"

Sky shrugged her shoulders. "I don't know. I've never known one intimate—that is, close up. Why's Holly so worried about her reputation as a business woman?" she added abruptly.

"Don't worry about Holly. She's got a great business sense; she just feels guilty about causing some damage last season when Kevin and Drew got into an argument over her. She was trying to sell the Bancroft bogs to a developer."

Sky smiled. "Obviously Drew talked her out of it." Their eyes met again, and his glance suspended her heartbeat. "She never bargained on the persuasive powers of the Branigan brothers. I could have told her a thing or two. And the rest of you, Ryan? Everybody healthy and happy?"

"For the most part," he said, lapsing into silence.

Sky turned and put the meat loaf in the oven and stared inside until her face was hot. She added some potatoes and then turned back. Thirteen years had given Ryan the beginning of crow's feet and deepened the crease between his eyebrows but not an extra pound had been added to his six-foot-two-inch frame. Time seemed to have worn away most of the defiance, too, and smoothed the rough edges as if he'd made peace with himself. He closed his eyes the way he used to just before he'd lean forward to brush her lips with his. She'd ceased to be affected by appreciative glances long ago; it was a shock to discover that Ryan Branigan could stir the waters all over again.

"I'd forgotten how tall you are," he said quietly, "but I'd have recognized you anywhere, even in waders across that bog."

Sky's attention was diverted to the mudroom door, which was being pushed open without a knock. A child in blue overalls came into the kitchen. She was a mass of freckles and strawberry-blond hair under a big red plastic fireman's hat that she held on her head with her hand as she looked up at Ryan. "You said you'd be right out! Mommy and Suzanne are waiting," she complained.

Ryan smiled and scooped her up. "I'm sorry, Katey. This is the friend I was telling you about, Janey—" he paused "—sorry, I can't remember."

"Cunningham," Sky added.

"Mrs. Cunningham," Ryan said, "and this is Kathleen Ryan Branigan. Kathleen Ryan was my mother's maiden name. Sean's a firefighter, and Katey and her sister have been on a tour of the station across the street."

"Come on," the child said. "You told Mommy five minutes. I'm hungry."

Ryan laughed. "Okay, let's go."

Sky walked to the door and held it open for them, trying to ignore the ache in her chest.

Under the enormous hat, Katey whispered, "Ask her."

Ryan said, "Hush!"

Nevertheless, Katey slung her arm around Ryan's neck and looked at Sky. "Mommy says if you're so rich, how come you're picking cranberries for Aunt Holly?"

Sky laughed out loud at Ryan's mortified expression. "Lord, Katey," he muttered.

"Tell your Mommy it's a small cash flow problem, and I thought it might be fun."

"Oh," she said. "Mommy says you used to be his girlfriend." This time she looked right into Ryan's face with a childish inquisitiveness that made him flush.

"That's right," Sky told her. "One summer I was his girlfriend. I was very lucky, too; every girl in Millbrook wanted to be his girlfriend in those days."

"And on that note, we're leaving," Ryan announced, "Before Katey gets me in any deeper. Take care of yourself, Sky."

"I will." She went into the driveway with them and stayed in the chilly October night long enough to watch the man and child cross the common under the streetlights. A station wagon sat at the parking lot of the fire station, and Sky could just make out the darkened shapes bending over and getting in.

"Good for you," Sky whispered in the dark, brushing back the melancholy and sense of loss. "At least one of us has done it right."

Holly's waders were a better fit, and Sky finished up her week's worth of harvesting in them. While she worked with the Mendes brothers out by Duxbury Road, she came to terms with the fact that she couldn't get Ryan off her mind. She cheered herself with the continual, silent lecture that schoolgirl crushes were seldom fatal, even at thirty-one. Sooner or later all the heart-pounding, adrenaline-pumping infatuation would dull. Her hormones would return to normal, and his appeal would fade. Wouldn't it? She wished he'd lost some of it during the past thirteen years.

Sooner or later her palms would stay dry when she saw a truck with the Branigan logo on the side. Her pulse wouldn't rush in her ears every time a patrol car cruised down Main Street. Sooner or later—hopefully sooner. Adolescent fantasizing wasn't particularly becoming at her age.

At the end of the week, with Jake due, Sky took the last of her wages from Holly. They'd finished at Duxbury Road and the bogs on Holly's property, which bordered the Branigan homestead. The only brother Sky met, however, was Drew, who shook her hand heartily and joked about the accident.

"I wish I could extend more hospitality," Holly complained when Sky returned her waders. "When you're back for good after Christmas, we'll get together."

"I'd like that," Sky said.

"Good. It's just that this is a frantic time of year. Everybody's exhausted. The men are up all night monitoring the bogs every time there's a frost warning, checking the sprinklers and pump houses. We added so much this season..." She shook her head. "They're at each other's throats from the stress."

Sky looked out at the flooded bog, this one bordered by neat rows of apple trees. A barn broke the gentle rise of lawn from where they stood to the Bancroft house on the crest of the hill. "I've never been in Millbrook except in summer. Fall is beautiful."

"I think so, too. I wish Drew had time to enjoy it. He and Ryan are trying to get some time to hunt, but even that's probably going to get scrapped with Ryan's schedule."

Sky was anxious to listen to the bits and pieces that made up his life. "Does he work with the others, besides his police work?"

Holly nodded. "He and Sean work the equivalent of two jobs this time of year, but Ryan wasn't supposed to be on assignment. He's a P.I., permanent police intermittent—that means he fills in, and takes extra duty. Somebody's out on disability now, so Ryan got called."

"Couldn't he decline till the season's over?"

Holly smiled. "He loves the work. That's what worries Kevin and Drew. Millbrook wants another full-time officer; the chief's asking the Finance Committee for the position and salary, and it'll all come up at town meeting in February. If it gets approved, then Ryan will have to put his name on the list or lose the position. It's a little complicated, but what it boils down to is that as a P.I. you can turn down permanent assignment three times; after that you either accept or that's the end. Ryan's come down to the wire. He's at the top of the qualifying list from the civil service exam. I think he really wants it.''

"But his brothers don't?''

"Drew and Kevin want him back in the business full-time. We've expanded so much this year. They really need him, and he's the only one left. Jody's a lawyer, and Matt's in his last years of medical school. Doctor, lawyer, fire fighter, cop, we've got a little of everything, but what we really need, especially if I'm going to concentrate on being a mother, is another cranberry grower. Kevin's pushing him, maybe too hard. I'm afraid Ryan will say no just out of spite.''

"So Kevin's still head of the clan,'' Sky commented.

"And likely to stay that way. The cranberry bogs are his life, unlike the younger brothers'. They're what make him tick. Drew, too—and me, much to my surprise.'' Holly walked Sky to her car. "You come back, and we'll get together like normal people, before the baby comes.''

They parted, promising to keep in touch. Holly's warmth was infectious, and the scenery was breathtaking. It was a heady combination for somebody trying to keep old feelings at bay. Still, Sky wanted nothing more than to jump into country life with both feet. But she'd keep her former crush on the periphery. She had to.

Her brother Jake arrived from Manhattan Friday night, gave her a big hug and some back-handed encouragement. "Better you than me. There are times I'm glad I'm the youngest.''

"It'll never be just mine, Jake. I'm putting it back into shape for all of us, even your kids some day. And I certainly expect some long visits here. No more Palm Beach reunions. We'll make Gram and Mother come to Mill-brook next Christmas.''

Jake laughed at her. "Don't lose sight of how this got to be yours in the first place."

"Default? So be it. I'm anxious to dig right in."

"Does Mark know you're moving here?" Jake asked.

"Last I heard from my dear ex-husband, he was engaged to a divorced mother of three. I'm sure he doesn't want to have any more to do with me now than he did the last two years of what he pretended was a marriage. I didn't ask for a dime, and what's mine is in storage. He doesn't need to know. Besides, he's got the Florida address and Mt. Vernon Street, too. Don't worry about Mark; I certainly don't."

"You don't even sound bitter anymore. That's healthy."

"I'm not bitter, and I'm very healthy. Now come and take a look at this ark and give me some brotherly, investment banker sort of advice." Sky turned her back and led him on a meandering tour that wound through the stately parlor, dining room, butler's pantry and library on the first floor up to the four bedrooms and sitting rooms on the second. "The plumbing's fine, and the furnace has been well maintained all these years. The radiators work perfectly, too. The real needs are cosmetic, and that's my specialty."

Jake listened. "Schuyler House definitely needs your touch."

"I'm going back to my maiden name, by the way. Might as well be a Schuyler again if I'm going to be its tenant."

Saturday, she and Jake spent the morning raking leaves from under the beech tree that hung over the iron fence and took up the corner of the front lawn. Both sides of the property were hedged in with lilac bushes over six feet

tall and thick as evergreens. As they dragged the plastic
garbage bags to the back of Jake's car, squad car 136
drove by. Sky waved and Ryan waved back. She did her
best to hide the excitement something so insignificant
could produce.

"Who's the cop?" Jake asked as they drove the ref-
use to the town dump.

"Ryan Branigan. I dated him one summer. You were
away at camp."

"The cranberry Branigan? Mom was still clutching the
drapes long after she shipped you off to Hungary."

"Austria, come on, Jake!"

"Seriously. Dad kept telling her to calm down. He said
you'd probably been a lot safer in the pickup truck than
you would have been in the back seat of one of your
preppy's station wagons." He laughed and patted her
knee. "It was great having you three years ahead of me.
Kind of paved the way."

Sky shook her head and looked out her window at the
passing foliage as they drove to the dump.

Sky left Millbrook as quietly as she'd arrived. No fan-
fare, no goodbyes beyond what she'd shared with Holly
at Bittersweet Bogs. Jake gave her hearty approval and
left for New York on Sunday morning after they'd
walked across the common to an early service at the First
Parish Church. Afterward they stood on the steps and
looked across the park.

"Stately," Jake said.

"Majestic. Good colonial lines. A proud heritage,"
Sky replied.

"A white elephant only a relative would love. You're
the one Sky, though. If anybody can make a go of this,
it's you, out here in the wilderness."

"I'm an hour from Boston! You just long for the feel of concrete under your Guccis. You take the Upper East Side, Jake, I'll take the cranberry country."

"It's a deal," he said. "Any delis open? I've got a sudden hankering for *The Times* and some bagels."

She spent the better part of November hunting down decorators in Boston who were willing to consult on a project so far south and finally found the ideal one. Ralph Sheilds had a firm footing in the nineteenth century but a flare for the twentieth. His suggestions were right on the mark, and his breezy manner suited Sky perfectly. It was a match made over Audubon prints and cabbage-rose chintz.

Through the Society of the Preservation of New England Antiquities, she was given the names of half a dozen tradesmen who specialized in restoration, all within an easy commute. With the historic nature of Plymouth County surrounding Millbrook, she found masons and painters and master carpenters schooled in exactly what she needed. She made all the arrangements from the Beacon Hill town house on Mt. Vernon Street, which was as close to what she considered home as any of the houses the Greenleafs and Schuylers owned.

From there the family attorney arranged to have her credit, name and all accounts reverted to Jane Greenleaf Schuyler. The trust fund was in order, and a checking account was set up at the Millbrook Trust Company. She left for Thanksgiving in Palm Beach, wishing it were the raw winds of Millbrook. It seemed that life, or at least Chapter Two, was about to begin.

Florida had a spell of perfect weather between the holidays, and Sky found that if she immersed herself in swatch books of fabric and wallpaper samples, back issues of *Architectural Digest* and *Colonial Homes* while she lolled around the pool, she didn't fantasize about blue uniforms or cable-knit sweaters or the way the Branigan house and its outbuildings looked in the autumn light at the edge of the crimson bogs. Schuyler House gave her focus, something most of her life had lacked. It was waiting, friends were waiting, and there would be roots, at last.

She streaked her hair with lemon juice and lavished gifts on everyone at Christmas, now that her finances were in order. She'd been the dutiful daughter but declined the invitation to extend the visit till New Year's Day. With hugs and tears she kissed her mother and grandmother goodbye, and flew with Jake and his family to New York and hopped the Shuttle to Logan airport. She spent the night of December twenty-seventh in Boston and arrived in Millbrook at lunch on the twenty-eighth. The general store next to the post office was having a sale on Christmas decorations, and she bought white-flamed electric candles for the front windows of her house and made herself a wreath for the door. Better late than never. It would be the last Christmas Schuyler House was dark during the holidays.

Four

——

While the furnace groaned into operation and the radiators clanked, Sky rubbed her arms in her lavender parka and fed the wood stove. The van with all of her material possessions arrived at two, the remnants of six years of marriage were unloaded through the arched Palladian doorway into the proper rooms and finished up by dark.

She took the Mercedes and bought enough food to fill her pantries, no longer needing to stretch the harvesting money. There were a few pieces of mail waiting at the post office, and she sifted through what was mostly junk mail over a barrel in the corner. The only one that held her interest was an invitation addressed, curiously enough, to Mr. and Mrs. Jake Cunningham. She turned it in her hand and opened it. It was an invitation to a New Year's Eve supper at the Santé Restaurant in Plymouth from Holly and Drew with a quick handwritten note along the bottom. *If you and your husband are in town yet, please join us. We'd love to make this an informal welcome!*

An hour later she was on the phone. "Holly, it's Sky. I'm back and I got your invitation."

"Welcome back," Holly broke in immediately. "Please say you'll come. It'll just be family and friends, nothing too big. It's a nice chance to introduce Jake to everybody."

"Holly!" When she was quiet, Sky laughed. "There's been a mistake. Jake's my younger brother, John Hobart Schuyler the third. As a matter of fact, I'm divorced. That's part of the reason I'm tackling the house."

"You are? Ryan said you were by yourself until your husband joined you. Boy, is he in for a surprise."

"Holly, please. I appreciate the invitation, but I haven't even unpacked yet. I'm not sure I'm up for New Year's Eve just yet."

"Nonsense. This isn't a date sort of thing. Matt's bringing both the girls he shares an apartment with in Boston, and Jody's coming single. It's really just family, and it'll be fun. Everybody's dying to see you again. We go right past your house. Drew and I can pick you up. Say yes."

"I don't know."

"That isn't *yes*."

"All right, yes! You're as persuasive as that family you hang around with."

Holly laughed. "I have to be. Anne and I are the only women, so far, that is. She has been wanting to apologize for her daughter's comments last October."

"Katey? She was adorable."

"Well, you can tell her yourself—Anne, that is. See you about eight or so on New Year's Eve."

Sky hung up, not sure whether she should be buoyed or not by the obvious sense that she was welcome even in their family celebrations. Anne and Ryan must have a wonderful relationship, she mused, reminding herself that for all its intensity, her fling with him had been just a few short weeks at a very young age.

On the afternoon of the party, she was still unpacking, but most of her clothes now hung in the bedroom closets, a twentieth century addition to the upstairs chambers. Her room was papered with cabbage roses and held a mix of wicker and mahogany that had sat in the same positions for fifty years. Sky had decided not to change it though she added her own fresh linens and feathery duvet, which she'd come to love in Austria.

She sat on the edge of the bed as she dressed, wrapped in a comforting sense of continuity. Schuyler House was inhabited only by her, but every room was crammed with memories.

Sky couldn't decide what to wear. She didn't want to upstage the very people she wanted for friends, yet her looks tended to make whatever she wore seem dramatic. She finally settled on an ice-blue crushed-velvet chemise-style dress, belted with a gold chain, and turned the collar up under her lemon-brightened hair. The mass of curls shone in a thousand shades of yellows and golds. Sky looked every inch the classic beauty she'd always been.

After she dusted eye shadow on her lids and brushed gloss on her mouth, she went downstairs to wait. There wasn't a room worth receiving anyone in yet, except the library, which she wasn't planning to change. She was sitting there, on the deep leather chesterfield sofa, when the brass knocker's sharp rap brought her to her feet.

She went through the dimly lit foyer to the front door and pulled it wide. Sky was greeted by a wintery blast, drifting snow and Ryan Branigan. "Happy New Year," he said.

"Why is it that every time I expect Holly, I find you at the door?"

The green eyes that made him look so deceptively innocent were wide, and his smile was so broad it deepened the creases at his mouth. "Just lucky, I guess."

Pleasure and a look of such sensuous intensity played over his features that Sky finally put her hand to the hollow of her neck, thinking perhaps she'd forgotten to fasten the button. She prayed the expression on her own face was less emotionally revealing. There was no longer any place for that kind of response, and she'd tell him if she had to.

Ryan had on a navy cashmere dress coat with the collar turned up against the cold, and his hair and shoulders were damp with fallen snow. There was nothing else visible except a slice of white oxford shirt and the knot of a maroon tie imprinted with holly sprigs. She tried to quiet the pounding in her chest, balling her fists to keep from brushing the flakes of snow off his coat.

"Car's all warmed up," he said, "but you might want boots." He looked askance at her delicate heels.

She smiled and opened the closet. "I'll chance it."

He helped her into her quilted coat, waited while she closed the front door behind them and then swooped her into his arms for the short walk to the idling Bronco.

"Ryan, put me down!"

He simply laughed and carried her as easily as if she'd been half his size rather than the statuesque woman she was. "Can't have you spending the evening with soaking feet."

"Ryan—"

He opened the passenger door and put her in. The car was empty. When he'd gotten behind the wheel and they were driving away from the village, she turned and looked at him.

"Where's your family?" she asked.

"At Santé or on their way, just the way we are."

Sky knew evasion when she heard it, and her mood began to change. "Holly was supposed to pick me up."

He nodded. "I was at their house when you called and volunteered for the assignment the minute I found out you didn't have a husband."

She shook her head and looked through the windshield as the wipers batted away the snow. "Why did you think that?"

He laughed. "Who else would Jake have been? You said your name was Cunningham and you kept dropping Jake's. I saw the two of you raking leaves and stuffing them into the Volvo with New York plates...."

It was her turn to laugh. "You jumped to pretty big conclusions. I've been in Atlanta, not New York, for one thing. Jake lives in Manhattan."

"Your Mercedes has Massachusetts plates."

"Brand new."

"Well, pretty sloppy piece of detective work, I guess," Ryan added.

"I guess!"

"Did I meet Jake?"

"That summer? No, he was at camp. And I'm dropping the *Cunningham*. I might as well use *Schuyler* again. It's been two years."

"How long were you married?"

Sky blanched at the personal turn in the conversation. "Forever. I met Mark my senior year. He was at U. Va.

in law school and then he went back to his father's firm in Atlanta.''

"Big bucks?" Ryan asked irreverently.

Sky smiled. "Big bucks, big mistake."

"You don't strike me as the wife of an Atlanta attorney, somehow. I can't imagine you behaving yourself. Maybe it was seeing you in the waders in my bog, half drowned."

"Well, I didn't strike Mark as the wife of an Atlanta attorney, either," she replied bitterly. "And you hardly strike me as a police officer, so I guess we're even."

"I'm sorry," Ryan said finally. "I didn't mean to hit a nerve. That was a stupid thing to say about behaving yourself. You know what I meant."

Did she? "Never mind. I shouldn't have said that about being a police officer," Sky countered.

"You're not alone on that score, Janey, believe me."

It seemed impolite to add how much she'd learned from Holly. It was a Branigan quarrel, not hers. "Did Holly tell you about the boys?" he added, as if he'd read her mind.

"I don't think so," she replied, wondering for a moment how many children he could claim.

"Through the Police League, I work with a bunch of teenagers. I figure I know as much about kids in trouble as anybody."

The dark countryside was giving way to the lights of Plymouth's outlying neighborhoods, and she watched the illumination play over his handsome face. It was full of enthusiasm.

"You weren't ever in real trouble, Ryan," she said.

"I came damn close even with Peter breathing down my neck and Kevin playing Big Brother. Twelve's a hell of an age to lose your parents Sky; I felt like I was just supposed to hang tough." He shook his head. "It was my fault. I should have let somebody know the pain I was in, I guess. Instead I got angry and mean and quiet."

"I remember the quiet," Sky said softly.

"I bet you do. By the time I got into my teens, I just wanted to play by my own rules."

"And do you?"

"Pretty much. That's where all the friction comes from right now. I love my family, but I just don't know if I want them as partners. I just don't know."

"And you're running out of time?"

He pulled the Bronco into the small parking lot for the intimate French restaurant. "I sure am."

When he'd turned off the ignition, she smiled again. "I'll bet you're wonderful with teenagers, Ryan. They're lucky to have you."

"Thanks," he said and got out of the vehicle. The snow was beginning to stick, and the lawn was covered with a thin white layer as light as powdered sugar. The path and paving were clear, however, and she insisted on walking to the door.

Once inside, they were greeted by an attractive woman, who gave Ryan a kiss and shook Sky's hand. "Welcome to Santé," she said. "I'm Andi Carter."

"Jane Cunningham. No! I'm Jane Schuyler—just not used to saying it yet."

Andi laughed. "We've met, but you probably don't remember. The night Kevin and Drew came home and found you and Ryan in the house alone with the beer..."

Sky's eyes widened. "You were Drew's date!"

Ryan took Sky's coat. "Andi lectured me all night on alcohol and inhibitions, wise older woman that she was."

"Funny, I got the same lecture from Kevin, all the way home," Sky added.

Andi pointed to the staircase. "I married Drew's best friend. David's upstairs, now. You two go on up and join the party. I'll see you shortly."

Sky looked at Ryan, trying not to let her eyes linger over the navy blazer and flannel slacks or the casual way he put a hand into his pocket. Change jingled as they climbed the stairs. Holiday music played softly as the sound of voices drifted down to her. The hair along the nape of her neck prickled. Ryan was a foot behind her and staring; she could feel it.

At the top, she paused, aware that her arrival had hushed the room. It was set with half a dozen candle-lit tables arranged intimately. To the left a buffet was waiting with a well-stocked bar. The room was cozy and set as though the Carters were giving a private dinner party every night they were open.

The attention made Sky lift her chin and move confidently into the room, velvet rustling around her knees. If Ryan had been watching her bottom as she'd mounted the stairs, she'd never know. Every inch the gentleman now, he came up beside her and nodded to Drew. Holly waved, but the first to reach them was the redheaded woman whose photo Sky had seen in Ryan's wallet.

"Sky? I'm Anne Branigan, and I've been waiting for two months to meet you and apologize for Katey's remarks!" Her fair complexion colored to almost the same shade as her hair.

Sky looked at Ryan, then back at Anne. "I'm sure it seemed silly being a day laborer, but it seemed like the quickest way to earn some cash till all the paperwork came through from Boston. I thought your daughter was adorable, though."

Sky paused, wanting desperately to sound sincere. The melancholy ache began again behind her breast bone. A friendship with Holly was one thing, but until her internal organs started to behave themselves, Sky knew that being close to Anne would be impossible. Watching her with Ryan seemed suddenly unbearable. In a flash of unexpected insight, Sky realized that Ryan still meant too much for her to play the role of an old friend. She would get through the night and get out of his life.

She looked at Anne. "I understand Kate and Ryan are both named for Ryan's mother."

"Yes. Kathleen Ryan. She was a wonderful woman." Anne turned then and motioned forward a group of three. "Sky, I don't know if you ever met Matt, but here he is. This is Nancy Reed and Erin O'Connor who share an apartment with him in Boston. Nancy and Matt are medical students, and Erin's a nurse."

Sky was glad of the change of subject, and when Anne drifted away, she focused on the youngest Branigan and his medical partners. They talked about Back Bay and Beacon Hill and the advantages of having a male in residence. "Even my father approves," Erin commented. "And he's old school, if ever there was one. We've got great rooftop view on Marlborough Street. You'll have to come by."

Sky said she would. Holly joined the group, but when Erin mentioned she was an obstetrical nurse teaching childbirth classes, the ensuing conversation about breast feeding left Sky with nothing to add.

When Ryan went to get her a drink, Kevin came up and engulfed her with a bear hug, welcoming her back. The Branigans all had a strong family resemblance, and Kevin seemed more a contemporary and less of a father figure now that they were all adults.

She moved from Kevin to Jody, the lawyer, and finally to Sean, Drew's twin. Ryan and Anne caught up with her there as she talked about her house. "I admire you so much," Anne said softly. "I hate to see the district deteriorate. It's a special part of Millbrook, and your house is fabulous."

Sky smiled, concentrating on the impersonal conversation as she sipped the drink Ryan handed her. "I'll have you over when the renovations are finished. You should have come tonight to pick me up. I'm afraid it's about to be torn apart this week. You know, Anne, I don't even know where you and Ryan live."

Anne gave Ryan a humorous look. "Drew and Holly are on the hill in the Bancroft house, Ryan and Kevin still share the main house, and Sean and I built the new saltbox on the other side of the bogs. Have you been out?"

Sky blinked and digested the implication. She stared at Ryan, then at Anne and finally at Sean. "Anne, are you married to Sean?"

The redhead laughed. "Am I ever. Twelve years, and until Drew finally talked Holly into the idea, I thought I'd be the only female on the property. At least Sean and I have daughters."

Sky knew she was flushed. She also knew Ryan was staring at her.

"Sky," he said, cocking his head. "All this time you've thought Anne and I—"

The color seeped up from her neck. "Well, yes. I mean, Katey said—"

Anne put her arm through Sean's. "It's tough enough putting up with this one; Ryan would be more than I could handle."

"Kate's my goddaughter," Ryan added.

An emotional weight was lifted from Sky. "I see," she whispered and raised her bourbon to her lips. It went down like liquid heat.

Five

The sense of relief never left Sky. She was giddy with it, and she grappled with restraint. It made her wit sharp and her appetite small as she mingled and nibbled at hors d'oeuvres. She watched Ryan across the room, smiled when he talked, turned goose fleshed when he brushed by her. Ryan Branigan was a bachelor, single, unattached.

Anne and Sean moved with the easy affection of two people long and happily married. It was a pleasure watching them, too. The whole night was a pleasure. Erin was cute, Claudia, Kevin's date, was sultry, Holly was beautiful, even in a maternity wool dress. Kevin, Sean, Drew, Matt and Jody were handsome; and Ryan was gorgeous. Sky was besotted by her physical reactions to all of them; eighteen had never felt that good. There was a lot to be said for growing up.

Happiness and relief, pure as spring water, bubbled through her. She ached to flirt, to touch the back of his hand, a cuff, his cheek. She was a groupie at a rock concert, a fan at a Red Sox game, a cheerleader at homecoming, all wrapped up in a sophisticated package for Ryan to untie. Her euphoria was tempered slightly, however, by sharp words between Kevin and Ryan as they moved toward the buffet, obviously in the midst of a long-standing argument.

"Day after tomorrow," Kevin said, "we draw up the plans for the storage room and workshop. We're going to do it whether you're there or not, its dragged on long enough."

Ryan sighed. "You know damn well school's out and I'm working with the boys. If you want me, you'll have to take four seventeen-year-olds, too. As a matter of fact, they should be in on some of our work. They've got some shop experience."

"Forget it." Ryan chafed at Kevin's words but was quiet. He turned to get in line.

Sky felt as if she were eavesdropping and touched his arm. "Let's eat. Can't this wait till another time?"

He nodded. "God knows it's waited six months already."

Kevin's date took his arm, and they got their food and went to sit with Anne and Sean. Ryan and Sky helped themselves to thin slices of perfectly done roast beef, baby carrots and out-of-season beans and a spiced rice. As they moved from the buffet, Ryan lead the way to a vacant table by the window. "The real world can't always meet Kevin's schedule."

Sky put her plate on the white linen and let Ryan pull out her chair. "He's got a business to run."

Ryan sat across from her. "How well I know. I backed him into a corner this year, I admit it. I didn't expect this assignment, but it's my job, and I'm committed to those kids. They've had enough adults in and out of their lives. They need continuity. Never mind, it's not your fight. Eat your dinner.''

She lifted her fork and looked at Ryan as the candle flickered. His face was tight, determined; it was a look she recognized.

He leaned forward slightly. ''I love the way you look at me,'' he whispered. Her small talk dried up before it began. She turned and looked at the snow collecting in the mullions of the small-paned window and at Ryan's reflection, his eyes meeting hers in the glass.

The night went too fast. It was midnight before it had any right to be, and as David walked among the Branigans and filled the tulip glasses with his best champagne, Andi began the countdown. The mood was expectant, happy, as earlier tensions, if not forgotten, were at least put aside.

When Andi cried ''Happy New Year'' and went up on tiptoe to kiss David, everyone joined in. Sky looked at Ryan over her glass, and when she'd taken a sip, he took it from her and put it on the table. He put a hand on each of her shoulders and smiled at the velvety smoothness under his palms. His kiss was quick, firm and warm. ''That's the kiss you would have had if you'd been here with a husband named Jake.''

A smile played at the corners of Sky's mouth as she stared at him. Before she could reply his hands moved to her temples and he tilted her head. His mouth hesitated over hers, a hair's breadth away, then touched warmly, his lips slightly parted. The tip of his tongue ran along the velvet lining of her bottom lip. For months she had refused herself the luxury of trying to recall his kiss, but now her brain was unable to focus on anything other than the crackling response of her body.

She reminded herself of her surroundings, where she was and whom she was with. Where was decorum when you needed it? Her hands flew to his neck, up around his shoulders, and the moment the rest of her pressed against him, Ryan tensed, then crushed her close. Their mouths met, clung and finally parted. Ryan was quiet. She'd known he would be, but he smiled and slid one finger down her cheek and across her lips before they both turned to the rest of the family.

Hugs and kisses were exchanged all around and then it was over. As they left in the midst of thank-yous, Anne joked about leaving Ryan alone with his old love, and Sky wondered if she'd ever tell Sean's wife of her doubts.

The snow had deepened, and the ride home was slow and beautiful. The brothers Sky had spent the evening with were as different from one another emotionally as they were physically similar. Their taste in women, their temperaments, each bespoke total individuality. Sky wondered if Kevin recognized that. He and Ryan were the quiet ones, brooding sometimes, maybe too much alike.

Once they were back in Millbrook, Sky made conversation, watching the snow and the lights as Ryan drove around the common to Schuyler House. His nature intrigued her, as it always had, because it kept her off balance as few things in her pampered life had ever done.

Few men, if the truth be told, are comfortable with a woman whose beauty borders on flawless, especially if the woman is five feet eight inches tall. Fewer still, even if they matched her in stature and looks, had anything remotely resembling character under their own gleaming surface. The men in Sky's life who had drawn the best from what she had to offer, who had said *no* to her whims and *yes* to her courage and independence were precious few. At that moment she could think of three.

John H. Schuyler, Jr., her father, and Jake, his name-sake, were two. Ryan Branigan was the third.

They passed the church and the grocery store and the quiet fire station and came to rest in front of the white clapboard colonial. Ryan turned off the ignition in front of the iron fence with its thin cap of snow and looked at her. "I'll see you in," Ryan said.

You bet you will, a little voice said in her head. "That would be nice," she said out loud. Sky waited for him to come around and open the door, and this time, when he scooped her into his arms, she laughed and let him carry her up the snowy brick walk.

The lamp in the foyer was on, and once inside, Sky slipped out of her shoes and let Ryan hang up her coat. She handed him a second wooden hanger. "You'll stay for a nightcap?"

"I don't think so," he said matter-of-factly.

Instantly she changed her demeanor. Had she misread him or been so wrapped up in her own response that she'd been assuming the desire was mutual?

"Another time," he added.

She leaned back easily against the old wallpaper.

"This is all coming off tomorrow," she said to change the subject.

"The whole house?"

She nodded. "Room by room. I'm going to devote six months to it and then quit for a while. It'll be interesting to see how much clutter and chaos I can stand."

He cocked his head in that way of his and looked at her thoughtfully. "Have you worked at all these past years?"

Sky sighed. "I've done a lot of fund-raising and volunteer work, which took up my energy. Since Mark and I didn't have children, I had the time."

"What did you major in, back at Hadley?"

She looked at those sinfully green eyes watching her. "English Lit."

For a moment Ryan glanced at the wallpaper just to the left of her face, but then his eyes returned as if drawn to her. "After the army, I went to the University of Colorado."

"Really! I didn't know."

He gave her that languid smile. "It was an excuse to ski and put Kevin off a few more years. That's where I got interested in criminal justice."

Sky let herself simply look at him, seeing if she could find a sign of what lay behind those eyes. Before she could respond, he brushed her cheek with the knuckles of his hand. "That look has haunted me," he said suddenly. "The way you look right into my soul. You could always do that."

She smiled dreamily, her heart jumping. "I always liked what I saw. I still do."

"There've been a few scars since the last time you looked."

"Gives you character," Sky said easily. The desire to hold him was nearly unbearable. She shifted her bare feet on the wide pine floor.

"You were a dream that summer, Sky. Those weeks were a dream. It might be best to keep the dream the way we remember it." Ryan's voice was low, as if he might be overheard.

She put her hand on his cheek, afraid he might remove it. His hand closed around her wrist, but he kept it where it was. Desire shifted his features, and she kissed him the moment his eyes were closed. "That's the kiss you would have had tonight if you'd been with a wife named Anne," she said. He shook his head at her.

Sky knew in those moments that Ryan had been fighting as hard as she, and though the reason obviously wasn't Anne, his turmoil had yet to settle. Sky was also woman enough to know that standing within inches of each other wouldn't settle anything. "I'm going very soon," he said as he let go of her wrist and moved both hands over the velvet fabric at the hollow of her neck. His expression was tortured, and she closed her eyes so she couldn't see it, but the delicate weight of his hands made her sigh.

Sky knew an embrace was coming, and his arms, at last, closed around her, pulling her away from the wall. "Very soon," he moaned as she burrowed her arms under his topcoat and blazer, along the cotton-covered broadness of his back.

Sky's blood may have been blue, but it simmered with steam, like her red-blooded Irishman's. She filled the space between them with her soft, pliable self and swayed unconsciously as they kissed. He held her against his heart, his desire draining his self-control. There were too many memories and too little distance between them for the kiss to do more than stoke the feeling. She snuggled against him and massaged the small of his back with tiny strokes until a deep satisfied purr rumbled in his throat. His breathing was shallow and quick as he caught his breath and put some space between them again.

"Some things you never forget," he said, and he let go as quickly as he'd been quick to hold her. He lifted both his arms and pressed his open palms against the wall on either side of her. Restraint. It was as familiar as the kiss had been, something they'd mastered long ago but had no need for now. Ryan brought his head up and focused on the paper while she let her breathing settle. Had he pursued it, every inch of her would have said *yes*.

"Coffee?" she managed.

He exhaled deeply. "I don't think so."

"I grind my own Colombian..."

Ryan laughed softly and pushed himself away from the wall, his hands back at his sides.

"Mocha Java?" She shifted, as well, looking graceful, if mussed, and still playful. Ryan brought that out in her.

"Another time, Sky. I'd like that."

So most of him had been telling her. He may not have had a wife named Anne, but clearly there was someone or something else. Ryan Branigan wasn't one to hesitate unless there was a very good reason. He stood in front of her now, shifting, getting ready to leave. They moved to the door, and he turned.

"Velvet on you is—" He seemed to search for words.

"Dynamite?"

He laughed at her and ran his hand over her sleeve. "It picks up the light and falls...my God, it's sensual. Tonight, every time you turned, another part of you shone. You do shine, you know Sky. I think you're more beautiful as a woman than you were as a girl."

"What a lovely thing to say." And odd, Sky added silently. It was more of an opening conversation than one to close what he obviously didn't want to finish. "As a matter of fact, Ryan, it's a joy looking at you, too. It always was."

Pleasure danced across his face. Sky chose to hold that moment as a memory, and she opened the door. It was nearly two in the morning and well below freezing.

"Some night," he said as a goodbye, his breath coming in gray puffs.

She nodded. "Full of surprises. Thanks."

He kissed her quickly. "My pleasure."

When he'd turned to walk to the Bronco, Sky closed the door and stood with her velvet-covered back pressed against it, listening until the sound of the engine faded into the still New England night.

Sky woke up the next morning in a cocoon of warmth, snuggled into her duvet. Her bed was a tumble of designer sheets and fluffed pillows. A mass of disheveled curls peeked above the comforter. Sky stretched and smiled. Detective work lay ahead.

The sun was already above the bare maple branches, and the room was bright and filled with the deep rumbling of passing plows. Sky threw back the bedcovers and rubbed the goose bumps caused by the chilly air. It made her feel all the more alive. She slept in a nightshirt, which stopped well above the knees and was open at the neck. Billowing nightgowns inevitably tangled around her like a straight jacket as she slept. She grinned at her image in the mirror on the way to the bathroom and yanked the shirt over her head.

In the shower, with hot water cascading over her scalp and down between her breasts, she wondered if Ryan fantasized about what she slept in. Did men do that? Had her perfume lingered on his shirt last night? Had he slept in it like a lecherous eighteen-year-old? She closed her eyes and lifted her face to the nozzle. This was fun!

She spent the better part of New Year's Day in her paneled library, filling the shelves with her books and family photographs. This Christmas she'd been given her father's collection of first editions, and she arranged them carefully among the silver and leather-framed mementos.

The deep sofa faced a small fireplace, where she built a fire, starting with the discarded packing paper. At three-thirty, after hours of dusting treasured books'

spines, her mood was mellow, and she called Holly. A
male voice said hello.

"Drew?" Sky asked automatically.

"No, it's Ryan. I'll get him. Sky?"

"Yes, it's me. I was just calling to thank Holly for last
night." She tried not to sound breathless.

"Happy New Year. I hope it's a good one."

"Why thanks, I hope yours is, too." She considered
the implications while Holly was called to the phone.
Over the distant sound of televised football, Holly added
her greeting.

"I just wanted to thank you for talking me into join-
ing your family last night. It was wonderful. Please thank
the Carters, too. They did a fabulous job." If she em-
phasized the meal and the restaurant, maybe Holly
wouldn't pick up her sudden breathlessness or the reason for it.

"We'll do it again before the baby comes," Holly replied. "As a matter of fact, why don't you come out for
lunch tomorrow?"

"Tomorrow?" Over the background, which included
a sudden cheer, Sky tried to decide whether she'd interrupted a New Year's Day party and this invitation was to
make amends. She imagined Ryan on the couch, with his
arm slung around somebody else, and then chided herself for feeling that insecure, or that jealous.

She accepted. "My painters arrive in the morning, but
as soon as I get them started, I'll drive out."

Holly seemed delighted, and after a few more comments, Sky hung up. A friendship was developing, which
Sky felt instinctively would be a strong one, woman to
woman. She needed it, even though it might be complicated by the familial ties.

The temperature in Millbrook hovered in the forties and fifties, with bright sunlight. The New Year's Eve snow melted where it lay thinnest, leaving heaps along the curbs where the plows had left it. The next morning Sky stood at her bedroom window and looked out across the street on the common. Downstairs her preservation-approved painters had moved most of the parlor furniture into the dining room and draped the larger pieces. They were tackling the job of stripping the wallpaper. Sky liked the bustle and anticipation, and she hoped she'd still feel the same weeks from now when the novelty wore off.

At eleven, dressed for the weather in cords, a heavy turtleneck and oversize sweater under her lavender parka, she set out for Holly's. She smiled as she turned off the town road onto the lane marked Bancroft and Branigan. It sounded like a law firm or maybe a rock group. The acreage looked bare and open compared to her October visit when she'd been working on the bogs. Without the bright, thick foliage, the Branigan house was easy to see from the crest of Drew and Holly's hill. The tall pines that ran along the perimeter added green against the blue sky, and the white trunks of birches provided contrast at the edge of the pond. She got out of her car and looked over at the new saltbox, Anne and Sean's, then back to the collection of Branigan buildings and finally glanced around Holly's porch. There was a note stuck in the storm door saying Holly was down in the Branigan barn with Drew.

She could have walked, but opted to drive and turned the Mercedes down the sloping drive. Smoke curled from the chimney at Ryan and Kevin's, and a black Labrador retriever sat on the porch. The bogs, well beyond the lawn, were flooded, icy at the corners and newly sanded. It was all like something from a Currier and Ives print.

Sky pulled her car next to the Bronco and got out as Holly came from the barn. "You saw my note! I came down to see the plans Kevin has drawn up for the barn. Since this is off-season, they're going to build a workshop and storage system inside. Welcome to the homestead."

Sky smiled. "It really is quite a layout."

Holly looked at the handsome white house. "No matter where any of them are, it'll always be home base, I think. I didn't understand how much land could mean to you when I tried to sell off what had been Peter's." She pointed up to her own house.

"I had a terrifying chimney fire up there the week I arrived and discovered a Branigan—the enemy then, you understand—was not only a fire fighter but was the double of Drew. They insisted that I spend the night at the Branigan homestead and in Ryan's room, thinking he'd be with Johanna Dente, a sort of fiancée at the time. He came charging into the room at midnight, badge, gun and uniform. I swore they'd done it on purpose!"

"Sort of fiancée?"

Holly paused, then smiled slyly. "Very serious, a relationship of the eighties. Johanna did her thing, which happened to be banking, and Ryan did his. Unfortunately for Ryan, his police work, cranberry business and saving every delinquent in the county didn't leave a whole lot of time for Johanna. She called it quits at our wedding reception, as a matter of fact, last April."

Sky tried to look as though she were mildly interested, not memorizing every word. Poor Ryan, such anguish, she mused and wondered how much of that sting accounted for his backing off two nights previously. "That's too bad," she said out loud.

Holly nodded. "Knocked him cold, poor thing, just like a man. I could see it coming for months; she just got tired of waiting. Then again, I think deep down, if Ryan had really thought she was the one, he would have done something long before. I don't know. We've gotten very close since I jumped into their lives. I think I'm closest to him of all the brothers, though. Ryan holds a lot inside, just like Kevin. Drew's just the opposite. He swept me off my feet as if he knew I'd fall madly in love with him."

Sky smiled. "He was right, of course."

Holly shook her head. "Was he, ever. I'll say one thing for all of them, they're the most confident bunch of men in Plymouth County." She laughed. "I know you two meant something to each other once, even if you were just kids. Maybe Ryan needs to be swept off his own feet for once."

Sky smiled. "Maybe he does, and who better to sympathize than an old love who has known the agony of divorce." Her voice grew melodramatic. "Single but burned."

"Sadder but wiser," Holly added, "and it certainly would help pass the winter."

Six

They started toward the barn together, and Holly massaged her back as she walked. "This kiddo's doing handsprings, I swear!"

Sky laughed. "You and Drew didn't waste any time."

"Well, he's thirty-five and I'm thirty-one. We had no idea how long it might take to get pregnant. Ideally, I wanted to conceive sometime this year. It was a bit of a shock when I got pregnant the first month I tried. Thank heavens I'd always been careful till I was ready."

After thirteen years, a twinge of anguish still trickled through Sky. The irony of not being able to conceive once she had married Mark seemed just as well now, but was part of the strain of her floundering marriage from the start.

The dog arrived, nuzzled at their knees, and Holly bent to pat it. "Domino, let's go find your masters," she said, grabbing Sky's arm as she straightened up.

The barn was cavernous and cluttered. Kevin and Drew were in the left-hand side with tape measures and graph paper, among shop tables and tools of every description. They both waved a quick greeting. Domino trotted in their direction.

Heavy equipment was parked on the other side of the barn. A flatbed truck, a pickup and the water reel nudged each other. The pickup had its hood raised, and five heads came up to watch the women enter. One was Ryan's and he grinned. The four others belonged to the teenagers, each the size of a full-grown man. Ryan was dressed as they were: faded jeans, work boots, a stained vest over a thick wool sweater. He had everything but the bandanna, and Sky held back the urge to pounce on him.

"Hey, man, what a fox," one of the teenagers said to Ryan in a stage whisper as he watched Sky approach.

"Why, thank you," Sky replied, her best smile dazzling the teenager into incoherence. He turned scarlet.

"Some of my friends," Ryan said. "Eric, who does know how to compliment, Joe, Jason and Tony. This is Jane Schuyler."

"Sky," she added, shaking each of their greasy hands, careful to look each in their guarded eyes. "Giving the truck a tune-up?"

"Anything to keep us off the streets," Eric added.

"Resident wit, too," Ryan said.

Sky watched them work, watched Ryan joke and guide and teach. So love had dealt him a blow, too...strong, silent Ryan. The bigger they are...

"Egg on my face?" he said while he wiped his hands on a rag.

"I just enjoy watching you," she said honestly. He met her eyes and held the glance longer than was necessary.

"How about that lunch I promised you," Holly said, and Sky agreed. As she turned to leave, she looked back at Ryan and the boys.

"I've got a thirteen-year-old Mercedes you might like to look at," Sky said.

"No lie?" Jason responded.

She raised her hand. "Scout's honor."

"Totally awesome," Tony added.

Sky looked at Ryan. "I thought they might think so. What'd you say?"

Ryan looked amazed. "I'm due at the station at four, which gives us just enough time to finish this up. Would you consider bringing it back in the morning?"

Ah, another excuse to return. "Sure!" She could hardly wait.

Kevin sauntered over during the exchange and waited till they'd finished. "Look, we've got work to do. My truck's one thing, but the barn is not big enough to turn this into a trade school, Ryan."

They eyed each other evenly. "One lousy day, Kevin. We'll get this finished, and I'll get back to you. Don't sweat it." Tension and restraint hung in the air until Kevin announced he was going in for lunch and left the barn.

"Massive attitude problem," Eric mumbled.

"Forget it. Let's get this done." Ryan looked back at Sky. "Thanks."

"Don't mention it. I'll be back in the morning."

She had a leisurely lunch with Holly and a tour of the charming Greek Revival farmhouse so lovingly decorated during the past ten months. They talked the afternoon away, skimming topics from Holly's love of opera and her half-Italian heritage to the cranberry business and Sky's plans for her own homestead. At three-thirty there was a knock on the front door.

"I'm going to go stick a load in the washing machine," Holly chirped, already waddling toward the kitchen. "Would you answer it for me?"

Sky arched her eyebrows. "What?"

"I think it's Ryan," she called over her shoulder.

Sky crossed the living room to the small foyer and opened the door. "Officer Branigan?" He stood on the stoop in his blues and his leather jacket, all spit and polish. "Come in."

It would have been easier to joke if he hadn't been looking at her so intently. Up and down the green eyes traveled, not lustfully but almost wistfully. When she finally caught his glance, his lashes swept away the expression. "That was a generous offer. I just wanted to tell you that I'll watch them every second, but they are good mechanics. We'll just take a close look. They're a good bunch basically."

"Basically?"

"Neglected more than anything. Not enough father figures, and too much spare time, especially during vacations."

Sky gave herself the enjoyment of looking him over briefly and settled on his polished boot tops before raising her eyes. "You know, I would have picked Kevin for the one saving the world, not you."

"People change in thirteen years, Sky, in lots of ways."

"I like to think so, Ryan. We had a lot of growing up and running away to do. It seems we've both come home to roost."

He touched her hair. "Welcome back."

When he'd gone off to work, Sky wandered through the house in search of her elusive hostess. In the laundry room off the kitchen Holly was sipping herbal tea. The machine was running. Smiling, she lifted the lid. "A whole load, see?"

"Did you know he was coming over?"

"Whenever Drew's not home, Ryan checks on me on his way to the station. He thinks I'm going to go into labor and not bother to tell anybody."

"You're a month away," Sky said with a laugh.

"They are all a bunch of mother hens. So, how does he seem after all these years?"

Sky eyed her friend. "Who wants to know?"

Holly sipped and scooted Sky back into the kitchen. "The vibrations between you two could make a light bulb glow. I'm just a curious bystander enjoying the show."

Sky declined an offer of tea. "He seems thoughtful, strong willed as ever, restless or stressed, just the way I remembered him. Cautious, too, and that's new, very new." Sky looked around the kitchen. "Did I say gorgeous?"

Holly smiled. "He's a Branigan; that goes without saying."

"Cautious," Sky repeated to herself.

Holly shrugged. "Until the day before yesterday, he thought you were married. That might make a world of difference."

Sky got back to Schuyler House to find the parlor stripped and ready for priming. The first floor smelled of solvent and chemicals, which she masked by putting a chicken in the oven. Afterward she stood in the arched entrance of what would be a perfect formal room. Sky wanted to fill the house with friends, and now, after less than a week in town, she felt she was making some.

When the tradesmen returned in the morning, Sky stayed long enough to brew them a pot of coffee and get them started before she took the Mercedes to Ryan. Millbrook was bathed in gray, shadowless light from a neutral sky, warm enough for the remnants of the New Year's snow to puddle. The bogs shimmered as she drove down the hill, and a wind kicked up tiny waves over the plants.

Sky was dressed for the weather, and as always, she looked an incongruous blend of heavy clothes and a deep tropical tan. Eric appeared at the barn door and gave her a wave. "Drive her right in, Foxy," he called when she'd run the window down. Sky also caught the final comment. "Hey, Officer Branigan, your babe's here."

As she got out of the car, Ryan came over with the ever-present rag in his hands. "Hey, babe," he said. Sky raised her eyebrows. "Get out and make yourself at home. Kevin will be here shortly. Drew's gone with Holly to her OB check-up so he can listen to the fetal heartbeat. You mark my words, when that little Bancroft-Branigan arrives, Holly will sail right through. It's Drew we'll have to hold up."

"Just like a man," she countered, poking him playfully. "None of you as tough as you think you are. A little thing like childbirth turns you guys to putty."

"Watch it, Foxy. You're addressing an officer of the law, and it may surprise you to learn that as an EMT I've even delivered one."

"You!" She cocked her head.

He nodded. "Back seat of the cruiser in the parking lot of the hospital. We almost made it. Piece of cake, and I did *not* turn to putty!" Ryan took her arm and changed the subject, as if delivering babies were an everyday occurrence. "Come on over here; there's somebody I want you to meet."

On the other side of the truck, within hovering distance of the boys, was a girl about the same age. "Kim Morella, my friend Sky Schuyler. Kim's a friend of Eric's."

Eric's friend looked at Sky with the wary expression they all wore. She was punk from her haircut to her pegged pants and ankle socks, with makeup more suited to midnight than nine in the morning. Sky wondered if her teenage rebellion had ever been that extreme. "Hi, Kim," she said, holding out her hand.

"Hi," she replied, pulling a pack of cigarettes from her pocket.

Ryan's bark made Sky shift her attention. "No smoking in the barn! Either can the idea, or face the cold, cruel outside, Kim. Too dangerous."

Kim lit up and headed for the door, and Sky followed. "Eric," Sky called, and when she had his attention, she tossed him her keys. "Want to be in charge?"

"No kidding! I mean, awesome. Thanks!" When he'd pocketed the keys, Sky went outside and found Kim lounging against the Bronco, blowing smoke into the morning air.

Kim laughed. "He's really jacked about your car. That's all he talked about last night."

Sky watched Kim study her. "You go with Eric?"

Kim shrugged. "Sure. Nice tan. You been to Florida or something?"

"Yes. My family's down there."

"Yeah. So I guess you're rich and stuff."

Sky shook her head at Kim's complete lack of pretense. "Yes, I guess I am, Kim," Sky replied.

The teenager left the cigarette in her mouth as she talked, with her hands shoved deep into her pockets, and her shoulders hunched against the cold. "I can always tell. I mean not just the car. You talk rich, you know, and you have that look." She glanced back at the barn. "The cop's rich, too. He pretends he isn't, like he's just one of the guys and stuff, but everyone knows about the Branigans."

Sky smiled. "I knew him when we were both about your age. He was very much like Eric and the others. He's not pretending. Money or not, he cares about all of you." She paused while Kim ground the butt under her sneaker. "Do you guys like Ryan?"

Kim shrugged. "He's pretty hot for a cop."

"Hot, that's good?"

The girl smiled. "Sure. Hot, awesome, way cool. I don't know if he's way cool, but he's okay. The guys like him, for a cop. He kinda reminds me of Magnum P.I. or somebody. Pretty intense for an old guy."

"Old guy!"

"You know, thirty at least," Kim said. The cigarette finished, they went back into the warmth of the heated barn, which took the chill from both of them. For a long time Sky stood back and watched Ryan work with the group. Ryan Branigan, who delivered babies and saved delinquents, had kissed her twice like there was no tomorrow. He made her hands clammy and her heart race just by raising his head from the depths of her car's engine and looking at her. She looked back, thoroughly enjoying the exchanges that were beginning to speak volumes.

Maybe she should ask him to dinner. Maybe he'd ask her to a movie. Maybe they could just walk over to his house and tear their clothes off. Her cheeks were hot under her rich person's tan. Maybe she should just go home. She couldn't; they were tuning her car.

Sky went back outside and raised her face to the bitter wind. Are we having fun? she asked the cranberry bogs. Any other man would have been putty by now. She had handled passes when she was married and passes when she wasn't. She could say *no* without speaking and make a man feel as though he'd been complimented. The least this adult crush could do was try. A movie would be nice, a concert . . . hell, she'd settle for a tour of the police station. The icy winds blew off the water as she wondered what he slept in.

He looked at her as though he meant it. Just how much chasing was a nice girl supposed to do? How carefree and flirtatious did she have to be? Had banker Johanna made him so gun shy that he'd sworn off women altogether, or had his taste changed since he'd been eighteen?

Jane Schuyler knew vibes when she got them, though; even Holly had noticed. No, there was nothing wrong with Ryan Branigan's taste or Ryan Branigan's anything else, for that matter. It was just a matter of time. Women knew these things. After all, they were the ones with the intuition.

When the group had finished with her car, they broke for lunch. If ever Sky had wanted to pull a twenty-dollar bill from her wallet and send the little darlings off to McDonald's, it was then. But Millbrook didn't have fast-food outlets. Besides, Kevin had appeared, and Drew and Holly had returned. They all made sandwiches instead in Ryan's kitchen and ate in the family room. Even full of people, it was cozy and inviting, the way she'd remembered from their clandestine evenings as teenagers.

They'd added a wood stove and more recent photographs, and the couch was too firm to have been there before, but all of it was tantalizingly familiar. The boys engulfed their lunch and played with Domino and a yellow Labrador named Max, rousted from the hearth. Sky watched Kim study the surroundings. There was a sharpness to her glance, intelligence in her eyes. Over the couch was an endearing portrait of Kathleen Ryan Branigan and her six boys, which tugged at Sky even now. Kim looked at it and then at Kevin, Drew and Ryan.

Behind the drug-store makeup and moussed hair, a mind was working, a perceptive one. Kim stepped to the bookcase and traced the spines and their titles with her finger. Eric caught up with her in the corner, and Sky caught sight of his hand curving over her bottom. She swatted him away. "Not here, okay?"

"Later, babe," he whispered and turned. He looked disappointed that his friends had missed the scene.

When Sky finally found herself alone with Ryan, it was for no more than a moment when they crossed paths in the kitchen with dirty plates. She set hers next to the sink. He handed her the keys to the Mercedes. "You made their day, Foxy." His green eyes flashed.

"Did I, Branigan?" She stared right back. "And my engine's none the worse for it?"

His breath caught, and he studied a curl at her right ear. "Your engine will purr like a satisfied cat."

"Will it?" She loved the game!

"Absolutely. Will you bring it back tomorrow?"

Sky nodded, afraid that her voice would crack if she used it. Let them rotate the tires, tear off the exhaust system, whatever they wanted. It all meant more time with the master mechanic.

It would have been the perfect time to touch his hair, brush his jaw—a signal, she told herself. *He's standing there waiting for a signal.* She was flushed and flooded with an attack of self-consciousness, struck mute by the power of his physical presence and unable to flirt. She held her breath, so he wouldn't know how rapid and shallow it was, and turned sharply toward the sink as Drew and Kevin came into the room.

Sky's efforts to concentrate on her decorating once she'd returned to her house bordered on the valiant. She spent the evening curled up on the deep leather sofa with swatch books and samples, nothing for company but the television.

The next morning Kevin was in the barn measuring the walls for shelving and marking it on the graph paper when she arrived. He gave her a big hello. It was the final day for the boys, and Sky wondered if he and Ryan had called a truce. They were flip and friendly with each other.

Kim was there, too, with less mousse and makeup but more earrings. Diamond studs, two in each lobe, set off her black sweatshirt. Sky accompanied her on another cigarette break. "You hate it that I smoke, don't you."

"It's not doing you any good, and it's sure easier to quit now than it'll be later on."

Kim nodded. "Yeah, I know. The cop's always ridin' me about it, too."

"He quit," Sky offered.

Kim looked mildly surprised. "He was really—you know—kinda tough?"

"More like angry, fast, always in a hurry."

"Tough break, having his folks kick off. Was that what made him angry?"

Sky tried not to laugh at the lingo and the speed with which Kim got to the point. "Yes, I think it was terribly hard on all of them."

"I was lookin' at the picture in the house yesterday. Was I right about rich? Silver frames, leather books—

you can tell, you know. A place has a feel, just like a person who lives there. I bet he could have a Mercedes if he wanted one, and I bet you have lots of those books and stuff, too," Kim said.

"I guess you've got me pegged," Sky replied.

"They've got all those Shakespeare plays. I saw *Romeo and Juliet* and we read it in English last year."

Sky watched the animation in her face. "Did you like it?"

"Yeah. Pretty dumb to kill yourself over a boyfriend, though, even if your parents do hate him."

"Did Eric read it, too?"

"Nah. He was supposed to, but I had to tell him most of it. He liked the movie okay, really got off on the sword fights."

They turned as Ryan came out, hunching himself against the wind. "If you'd give that up you wouldn't have to come out here and freeze your buns off, Kimberly."

She saluted. "Yes, sir, Mr. Officer!" With a grin, Kim left for the barn.

Sky rubbed her hands together until Ryan pulled them into his. He dropped the key into her palms. "All done. You're a good sport."

It had been three days since the kiss, and her bottom lip tingled. "Kim is quite a girl. She's got a way of seeing the truth, no pretense, brutally honest, and all in slang."

He smiled. "She's no good for Eric. It's doing terrible things to his concentration."

"Hormone overdrive?" Sky said.

Ryan laughed out loud. "God, yes! So Foxy, how about a far-out dinner, some 'boss place' next week when I come off the four to midnight shift?"

Speaking of hormone overdrive? she was dying to ask. "Right on," she said instead. "I don't suppose you'd care to be specific, my calendar being heavy and all."

"Sunday?"

Four nights to go. "Sunday would be nice," she said. "About seven?"

"Sounds good. I'll pick you up, and you can give me a progress report."

Of course he was referring to her house. Nevertheless, Sky laughed.

Seven

As was her routine now, before dinner Sky stood in the doorway of the parlor to assess the progress. A shadeless lamp cast a harsh light into the room, bright enough for her to see the excellent quality of the craftsmanship. She skirted the scaffolding on which they'd worked on the ceiling and ran her finger over the dentil work on the mantle. It would all be beautiful.

She took a swatch book to bed with her and thumbed through the damask and chintz, stewing over choosing drapes and loving every minute of it. Holly, she knew, would have some suggestions and maybe Ryan too. After all, he and his brothers had been in charge of their house for twenty years. She'd make a point of asking him on Sunday. She fell asleep thinking about him. She'd been doing that a lot lately.

Sometime later she awoke from a deep sleep to the sound of silence. Sky lay frozen on her side, frightened

by the pounding in her chest and the racing of her pulse
in her ears. She tried to remember what she'd been
dreaming, feeling sure that it had been a nightmare,
something terrifying that had hurled her into conscious-
ness. She lay gasping in the dark. Her bedside clock read
12:07.

Her fingers curled around the edge of her comforter as
the seconds dragged and her heart began to slow. She
snuggled more deeply into the covers and laughed at her
imagination until a distant scraping caught her ears. She
froze again and stifled the sound in her throat. There was
a scraping, a shifting and then one long thud that
sounded like boards hitting the floor. The moment it had
started up again she'd recognized the sound. It was iden-
tical to what had registered in her sleep.

The staging, she thought frantically. Someone, not
expecting the chaos, had knocked down the staging in the
parlor. Without turning on her light, she eased herself
from the bed and tiptoed across the carpeting to the door.
She pressed her open palm over the pin-striped cotton of
her nightshirt, oblivious to the still, cold air, wrapped
around her bare legs. She tried to think. If there were
prowlers, maybe they thought the house was empty.
Maybe after all the racket they'd fled. Maybe they were
on the stairs and outside her door. Sky pressed her forehead against the door. Oh, God, she thought, there were
disadvantages to living alone.

Without opening the door, she went back to her bed,
sat down to steady herself and picked up the phone. In
the dim light from the window she made out the emergency number taped to the receiver and tapped it out.

"Millbrook Police, Officer Martin."

In a whisper she reported what had happened and told
the desk officer where she was. She hung up, still too

terrified to move but determined to get downstairs. It was nearly twelve-thirty, and Ryan would be off duty. Her longing for him now had nothing to do with passion.

She eased the wrought-iron Norfolk latch up with one hand on the door and one on the frame and tiptoed barefoot, not toward the front landing, but to the narrow back stairs that would take her to the mudroom. The unheated back passage was frigid, and drafts from the rattling window sent shivers through her as she made her way. Halfway down she stopped. Someone was pulling open the batten storm door, letting in light through the panes of the one it insulated. Sky jerked her head up, expecting the sound of a siren or the wash of blue dome lights from the patrol car. There was nothing but the wind.

Whoever it was tried the knob; she watched it turn and heard the rattle. She'd locked it and thrown the dead bolt below it before she went upstairs. Maybe the police had sent an unmarked car. She began to inch her way down the stairs. If she could reach the washer and dryer where there was enough shadow, then she could see without being seen.

She was on the bottom step when the tinkling sound of shattering glass made her gasp. The butt end of a service revolver slammed through the corner pane of the door's glass, followed by a gloved hand and an arm in a cotton sleeve. It was too late to play cops and robbers. She jumped forward and took a good look at the shadowy figure just as he caught sight of her. "Sky!"

She opened the door, stepped back from the glass and threw herself into Sean's arms. At that moment any Branigan could have played hero. He was in his fire fighter's uniform, coatless and cold. "Are you all right? Watch the glass!"

Together they moved to the dryer where he let go of her and turned back toward Ryan, who had been right behind him, the .357 Magnum still in his hand. "The parlor," she said. "There were noises enough to wake me up."

"Stay put," Ryan said, and it was then that sweeping blue light began to wash the mudroom and kitchen walls. He disappeared through the butler's pantry as she and Sean went into the kitchen. She heard him open the front door.

"You know, Holly threw herself into my arms, too, when I got called to her chimney fire. I could get used to this," Sean said.

Sky managed a smile. "How did you know," she whispered.

"Police scanner at the station. Ryan had just stopped in on his way home. We both ran across the street. I got worried when I didn't see any lights."

"I was afraid to turn them on." She looked at the pantry door as the sound of footsteps on the bare front staircase held her attention.

"They'll search the house," Sean said.

She nodded. "Shouldn't you go back?"

"In a minute. We consider this a community service."

Sky enjoyed the sense of relief Sean's words and authority gave her, and as her fear began to subside, she snapped on the kitchen light. It was then that she remembered she was only in her nightshirt. Sean looked as though he'd read her mind and pulled an ancient man's work shirt from its peg in the mudroom. She put it on, though it only covered as much as her sleepwear. She was warming herself at the wood stove when Ryan and two of his fellow officers came down the back stairs.

"Nothing anywhere," Ryan said. "Sean, thanks. I think we're all set. Sky, will you go through the rooms with us and see if anything's missing? It's kind of hard to tell, with everything draped and moved."

"Of course." She thanked Sean profusely and fifteen minutes later was doing the same for the police. As far as she could tell, everything was as she'd left it, and she told them so. "I make a habit of going into the parlor to check the work. Maybe I knocked those boards over myself."

"Might have even been your weight on the floor-boards," the sergeant added.

Sky hugged the shirt to her ribs. "I'm sorry to have bothered you."

"Listen," he joked, "we'd much rather have it turn out this way. Call anytime, keeps us busy." They left by way of the front door while Sky stood away from the draft in the doorframe of the library.

Ryan came back to her the moment the door was closed. The house was aglow now. "You're trembling," he said.

"It's just the cold."

"Might be shock." He grinned as if he were trying to cheer her.

She put her hand out. "Want to take my pulse?"

He did and arched his eyebrows. Could he really tell what he was doing to her by the tiny throbbing under his fingertips? "You're very frightened," he said seriously.

Partly, she thought. "Living alone does have disad-vantages."

"This the first time?" Ryan asked.

"No, but after the divorce I got a one-bedroom apart-ment. It's not quite the same thing. I think I'll feel better when I have more of a sense of the community, and the house, for that matter. Sean was wonderful to race across the street.''

Ryan nodded. "He would have whether I'd been there or not."

Sky looked away, thinking she should offer him coffee or something. They were sidestepping the issue of her going back up to bed and his going home.

"Ryan, would you stay till I—" she blurted out.

"Sky, would you like me to walk you back upstairs," he said simultaneously.

They laughed. "It's silly to be still frightened," she muttered. "I just thought you could turn out these lights for me, or maybe I'll just leave them on."

"I'll do it, of course."

She smiled at him, and again their glances lingered on each other. She saw him swallow, heard the soft squeak of leather from his jacket or boots. She didn't want to drop her glance to see where the squeak came from.

Deep as a well, she thought, even after all this time. He was the first to speak. "Can we lock the storm door in the mudroom?"

"Yes. It'll keep enough of the cold out. I'll have the pane fixed tomorrow."

"I'll do it," he replied, and she followed him as far as the kitchen. When the door was locked, he snapped off the lights, and they retraced their steps, their shoulders occasionally brushing as, inches apart, they moved through the house. "Let's get you up there" was all he said.

Sky climbed the stairs ahead of him and had the same prickly sensation as when he'd followed her at the Santé. She was all thighs under the work shirt, trying desperately to hold in the slivers of fear and hold back the waves of desire.

At the top of the stairs she hesitated. He bumped into her and put his hands on her shoulders in the darkened hallway. "It's okay, Sky. Isn't this the same bedroom where I threw pebbles against the window one night?"

"The very same." He did have a way of cheering her up. She let him snap on the light on the bedside table.

She stood next to him, hugging the shirt around her ribs. Reading her body language, he asked if she'd be okay.

She nodded, clenched her jaw and raised her eyes to look at him, but he became blurred. She blinked, but too many tears had escaped, and their precarious balance on her lower lid was lost. They slid down her cheeks. Fear, exhaustion, anger could have been the cause, or even the maddening effort to keep her unrequited desire at bay. Whatever the reason, she was beyond caring as she loosened her arms and pulled her sleeve over her eyes.

Whatever personal battle Ryan had been waging, whatever restraint he'd managed till now evaporated. He sighed. "I was always a sucker for tears."

"Please! I'm fine. Just go now, Ryan, I'll see you Sunday night."

He didn't go; he opened his arms. She shook her head, but while she did, he took off his outer jacket and dropped it on the chair. The holster followed and the boots, and her breath caught as he continued. She took off her work shirt, but he was already naked, and as she reached for the hem of her nightshirt, he closed his hand around hers. His breathing was rapid, and watching his chest expand made her knees weak.

"Let me, Sky," he whispered, and as quickly as he'd gotten out of his own clothes, he slid off her underpants. Sky closed her eyes as he ran his hands over her body. When his open palms had cupped her breasts, she put her head back. He kissed her throat and the shell of her ear. "Touch me, Sky," he moaned.

It happened with the speed with which long-glowing embers, blown suddenly white-hot, erupt into flames. She raised her arms and fell against him as he pulled off the nightshirt. Pressed together, they lingered and swayed and explored each other until the room was full of the sound of sighs, and their hearts hammered.

They fell into the depths of the bedcovers, their moans rising over shallow gasps like an incessant erotic melody, the rhythm carrying both of them. Desire illuminated his features as the hunger built until she was fearful that she couldn't satisfy it. She'd longed for this moment but never dreamed of its intensity. She was raw with her desire and awestruck by Ryan's as she saw in him what she felt in herself.

"No," she managed to gasp. "Not yet, I want it to be perfect. There's so much more..." A romantic illusion drifted through her; she wanted symphonies and slow-paced ecstasy.

"Next time," he groaned. "My God, I've wanted you since last October...since the bogs... I've been crazy with remembering. We can't wait, Sky. There's no more waiting."

The sweet agony reached its pinnacle as he whispered, and they finally shared their fervor. Instantly she cried out as she moved under him, with him, against him, unable and unwilling to slow down. She felt his breath catch in amazement as he deepened her rapture. Though he'd sworn he couldn't wait, he held back time and again, as if her joy was intensifying his. When he finally lost himself in her, he called her name. They spun mindlessly, perfectly through a tunnel of pleasure, locked in an eternal rhythm. As it subsided, Sky moved against him and let herself drift back to reality.

Ryan moved away for just long enough to snap off the light and bundle them under the covers.

Eight

It had seemed to be over as quickly as it had started, but every fiber of her body was satiated, calmed, and he was still a breath away.

The sharp jangle of her phone roused Sky at nine. She moved gingerly under the dead weight of Ryan's arm and picked up the receiver. It was the painter.

"You probably already guessed we wouldn't be down today, weather and all."

Sky was blinking and looking through the half-drawn shades. "Blizzard, I guess."

"Travelers' warning, anyway, storm watch and all that. We'll be back tomorrow."

"Fine," she replied sleepily. "See you then." When the phone was in the cradle, she hunched up on one elbow and looked out again. The view of Millbrook was a hazy study in black and white. The snow fell heavily and silently, and the lilac hedge was already heavy with it. As if to validate the snowy scene, a plow passed with a thunderous roar of clanging and scraping. "Hot damn," she whispered.

Ryan lay curled on his side, away from her. She snuggled back under the covers and pressed herself against the curve of his spine with her arm draped over him. He moaned softly. Cops and doctors could probably sleep through anything, she thought. Desire began its gentle spiral like the curl of smoke from a winter chimney. She was as satisfied as a hearth cat and smiling like a Cheshire.

Without moving another muscle, he slid his hand until it covered hers, and then with a more rapid motion he dragged it to his chest. "You faker," she cried, letting him move her hand down his chest, over the flat plane of his stomach and pelvic muscles to the destination Ryan had in mind.

"You're a genius at putting me to sleep," he murmured. "How about waking me up?"

"Like this?" She knelt beside him and watched his expression change as he watched her breasts respond to his exploration.

"You wanted more time, Sky, take all you want." Still on his back, he raised his hand and traced the outline of her tan with his index finger. He went over the slope of her breasts and cupped their weight in his hands. "Some tan, you must swim in next to nothing."

"Gram's pool is very private."

He murmured "Hmm," and came up on one elbow. Gently he pulled each butterscotch tip into his mouth, the gliding of his tongue driving her shoulders back. He stopped, and his breath on the moistened tips gave them gooseflesh. "You're beautiful, Sky," he whispered.

She moved her hands into his hair and held his head there, letting the purr in her chest register against his cheek. As she studied what heightened his desire and increased his pleasure, she realized he was doing the same thing.

"Perfectly beautiful," he repeated.

"Beautifully perfect," she replied.

"I did say something about next time, didn't I?" Ryan added.

"In the heat of the moment."

He raised his head to look out the window. "Might as well heat up these moments, too, don't you think?"

She smiled wickedly. "I'd rather not think, just now, if you don't mind."

"Was I giving you the impression that I minded?"

Sky's smile broadened, but she let her hands do the talking. She teased and flitted away, then wandered back to him only to have him repeat her taunts while he was poised over her. They spent the better part of the morning kicking back the covers. We were made for this, she thought. It was the first time Sky had ever made love while laughing, as the desperate need for fulfillment was replaced this time by humor and contentment.

She communicated with Ryan on a primal level. She saw his desire, felt the pleasure he found in her and thrilled to the knowledge that she could satisfy him. "Perfect," he kept whispering, her man of few words. But what words they were.

It became harder to concentrate on him as he concentrated on her. Here was a man worth watching, a man who said more in a glance, said more with a touch than most men did in an evening's worth of conversation. The impatience and longing, so volatile in both of them at eighteen, had been expressed. Curiosity had been satisfied. The itch had been scratched. What held them now on the snowy morning was happiness and mutual delight.

Whatever reservations Ryan had held were gone with the night. *Maybe I'm irresistible,* Sky thought. *Heaven knows, the man in my arms is.*

They made a late breakfast together, and while Sky served it, Ryan stoked the wood stove. He had on the work shirt she'd worn the night before and his uniform trousers. The boots and the rest of the paraphernalia sat on a kitchen chair. Ryan closed the door of the stove, washed his hands at the sink and wiped them playfully on the apron around her waist before he sat down.

"Delicious," he said.

"You haven't tasted anything yet." When he grinned at her, she added, "I'm talking about my cooking."

"I can dream."

Sky munched her toast. "Have there been dreams, Ryan?"

"Some. Maybe that's what brought me back to Millbrook from Colorado. Some dream that I'd fit in, that I belonged with the rest of them. You made me restless for more than what was laid out in front of me, Sky."

"Me?"

"You and everything you represented."

"But you're back," Sky answered thoughtfully.

He nodded. "So are you."

"Maybe I'm back because I wanted what I thought you had. Family, all in one place, roots, a sense of belonging to something. I got that from you. We're opposite sides of the same coin, you and I."

"Maybe we are," Ryan replied.

As they sat over a second cup of coffee, there was a rap at the mudroom door. Sky had on shoes, but she was still careful around the shattered glass near the back door. Kevin stood in the snow, bundled in a parka and knee-high gum-soled boots.

"Come on in," Sky said, conscious that she looked decidedly disheveled. "Looking for your brother?"

Kevin smiled back. "I knew where to find him. Actually, I'm here to tell you that I'll plow your driveway up to the Mercedes, and then if you'll move it, I'll do the rest." He looked past her to his brother. "Station called—they want double shift. Had enough sleep to work overtime?"

"I'll manage." Ryan went through the pantry to the library to use the phone as Sky offered Kevin a cup of coffee.

He took the mug. "Sean says everything turned out all right last night."

"Yes, thank goodness. Some boards against the wall fell. Kevin, it scared the life out of me. Frankly that's the reason Ryan—" She faltered as she looked at the eldest brother and then laughed at herself. "I was going to say that Ryan's staying here was initially because I was less than thrilled about being alone in the house for the rest of the night." She ran her fingers through her hair. "Honestly, Kevin, I feel as though you're going to lecture me, just the way you used to do!"

Kevin laughed good-naturedly. "The only warning I'd give you this time around is that Ryan's got too many irons in the fire already. Don't expect a lot of time with him right now. On the other hand, if you can put some fun in his life, it might sweeten his disposition some."

She laughed as they got to their feet. "I'll see what I can do."

Ryan came back from the library as Kevin went out to the truck. "I'm still parked at the fire station. Sky, let me get out of this uniform, and I'll come back and fix the broken glass and shovel what Kevin can't plow."

She cocked her head. "Branigan Blizzard Service? Shall I expect this every time it snows?"

He kissed her. "It's the least I can do."

While he was gone, Kevin plowed, and Sky moved her car into the carriage barn. Lightweight aluminum snow shovels hung on the wall with the garden tools, and by the time Ryan returned, dressed like a lumberjack, she was making a path from the driveway to the front door. The snow had stopped completely, and the wind had died, leaving Millbrook fluffy as it dug out from under.

Ryan went inside with an odd-sized piece of glass he'd brought with him. Sky watched him as he worked on the pane. *The rough edges of his adolescence had been polished smooth,* she thought. *He's not out to prove anything to anybody except himself. Let the rest of the world make him pensive and introspective; I'll make him laugh.*

When she'd finished her tasks, she went back inside, to where he worked. Skirting his project, she watched him finish up.

"The pane fits, but the caulking's too cold. Keep this room warm for a while. Good as new." He got to his feet. "I'm going home to bed, Foxy. I don't recall getting much sleep last night, and I'm due at the station at four. I'll work straight through till eight tomorrow morning."

And then? she wanted to ask. Instead she smiled.

When she saw him to the Bronco, he kissed her chilly mouth. "Somewhere along the way you turned into a hell of a woman, Sky. You have a way of satisfying a man's curiosity a thousand times over."

She laughed and ignored the twinge of confusion at his choice of words. So he saw her as the old flirt satisfying their curiosity. She'd always played life for laughs. This might well be no different. "Keep in touch," she murmured with a sideways glance, and before he could respond, she trotted back through the snow to the warmth of her house.

Like the rest of New England, Millbrook came back to life shortly after the snow stopped. Like a chick breaking through its shell, the city emerged from the snow: stores reopened, traffic came back, and mothers sighed with relief that school would resume in the morning. After lunch Sky built a snowman with a few of her youngest neighbors, piling the mounded body seven feet in the air so that it stood majestically at the edge of her iron fence. When they'd added branch arms, somebody's pipe and scarf, she rummaged through the mudroom for her father's old sou'wester hat from his foul-weather gear. It gave a nautical touch to the historic district.

She thought about Ryan snuggled in his own bed and wondered if he missed the feel of her. She wondered if she'd miss him when she climbed her own stairs. She ladled cocoa out to her helpers, and when they'd gone, she turned with renewed enthusiasm to her fabric samples. She slept fine that night, but had spent a long time looking at the pillow beside her before she'd snapped off the light.

The painting crew finished the molding and wainscot in the parlor the next day and set up the staging in the foyer in order to tackle the stairwell. Once they were out of the front room, Sky got busy with her plans for arranging the furniture. With an eye for decorating and an ear cocked for the phone, she busied herself with the upholstery samples. Ryan didn't call. Why would he, she chided herself. He'd worked all night, and he was sound asleep. If he wasn't sleeping, then he'd be helping Kevin and Drew. If he wasn't helping his brothers, then he'd be riding herd on Eric and the boys. She sighed. Surely his curiosity couldn't have been *that* satisfied. "Ring, damn it," she said to the phone, but it didn't.

Millbrook huddled against a cold snap, which was unusual for a town so close to the sea. It kept the snow deep and fresh for days. The common and everything that ringed it looked picture-book beautiful under the sunny skies and starry nights. But it was the starry nights that did her in. After three days and nights of silent phones, Sky decided to give a small "before" party to let friends see Schuyler House as it was. She owed Drew and Holly, Kevin and a date would be nice, and she could throw in Sean and Anne and Jody, too, if he were interested. She laughed at herself. All the friends she had in mind were related to the real reason she needed the excuse. She made her plans in front of the ll:00 p.m. news, curled up in the corner of the chesterfield.

First thing in the morning she'd call and issue the invitation. She smiled, feeling like a certain teenage tennis player who'd kept one eye on the boy pulling weeds or riding the mowing tractor at the country club.

She wasn't sleepy. Main Street was a fairyland, and impulsively she bundled up, locked the doors and headed for a moonlit stroll. The air was sharp, winter-brittle, and she had to inhale in little gasps that slapped her into alertness. What snow had melted during the day froze again by late afternoon on these short days, giving the common a crust that glittered like spilled sequins under the street lamps. It was bright enough to read by as she walked the shoveled sidewalk and listened to the crunch of packed snow beneath her boots.

Where Main Street crossed Pilgrim, she turned right, her hands deep in her pockets now, her Scandinavian cap well over her ears. My town, she thought, watching the darkened windows of the big, handsome houses. As she brought her glance back to the path she was walking, an all-too-familiar sensation rustled at the base of her skull. The quiet purr of a car engine came up alongside her. She turned her head to the left as the hood nosed into her peripheral vision. It was a squad car.

Sky stopped and peered into the passenger window as it was being rolled down. The incredibly handsome officer, all spit, polish and infectious grin, raised the index finger of his gloved hand as he eased across the seat and crooked it. She stepped closer.

"Yes, Officer?"

He licked his bottom lip. "Kind of late for a woman to be out alone."

She widened her eyes, her heart dancing. "Gee, how'd you know I was a woman under all these clothes?"

The grin softened to a smile. He leaned out from behind the steering wheel and tapped her chin. "There's a certain swagger to the hips, a lightness in the step; cops know these things."

"My, my, and I thought all they did was write tickets and keep kids off the streets."

"Kids and shivering women. You wouldn't, by any chance, be looking for a little action, seeing as it's nearly midnight and you seem to be walking toward the station?"

Sky looked ahead at the floodlit front of the police station half a block away. "Goodness, is it that late?" She looked back at him. "What do you know. Tell you what, Officer. Why don't you just drive this squad car back, check out, and I'll meet you in the familiar-looking

Bronco parked in the lot. I'm exhausted, and I sure could use a ride home."

"Babe," he replied, "I'd consider it my civic duty and a civilian honor."

Nine

Sky reached the brightly lit lot as Ryan got out of his patrol car. He threw her his keys and invited her into the station. She declined, and he disappeared inside alone.

In the few minutes she had to herself, she started the Bronco and drove around to the front door. From her perch behind the wheel, she caught sight of Ryan through the clear glass doors as he chatted to the officer at the front desk on his way out. She watched as he came toward her in his uniform and then slid over to let him drive.

"What's that sneaky little grin on your face for?" he asked as he got in.

"Truthfully?"

"You're addressing an officer of the law," Ryan reminded her in a dignified tone.

"Well, I was wondering if you ever get propositioned when you're dressed like that. You're just about the most gorgeous man I've ever seen, Ryan, in uniform and out, for that matter."

He was silent as they pulled into her driveway, and Sky peered at him to figure out his response. "Ryan Branigan, you're blushing!" she declared.

"Like hell," he muttered.

Sky leaned over and twisted on the interior light as he tried to swat her hand away. "Right into the roots of your silky black hair."

Ryan gave her a long, quizzical look, as though he had no idea what to do with her. Sky decided the women in his life had been either too reserved or too intimidated. She yanked her mittens off and drove her fingers into his hair before he could do more than grab her wrist. They sat like that for a moment, her hand on his temple while his was wrapped tightly around her cuff.

With his free hand he turned the light back off and cupped her head. The kiss was open, deep and full of exploration. They stayed locked together like teenagers, busy from the neck up, fogging the windows. When she caught her breath, she began to laugh. "I remember doing a lot of that out here, but it was a summer romance. We never had this many clothes on."

He pulled her hat off and watched her hair fall around her face. "Every inch of me feels like I'm down to nothing." He kissed her again until soft moans caught in her throat. "I love the sounds you make," he whispered.

With his arms still wrapped around her, Ryan continued. "I think I better come inside and check the house for prowlers."

"Oh, would you?" she cooed. "Even off duty you're such a hero." She could feel the silent laughter in his chest as he held her.

When she'd unlocked the back door and led him into the kitchen, Ryan took off his jacket. "The answer to your question is yes—I've been propositioned in uniform. It's kind of a phenomenon of the job. Some women have a thing for uniforms. It doesn't have anything to do with being—" he fumbled for a word "—with the way I look, with who I am."

Naive, she thought, or modest. "Well, Officer Branigan, I fully intend to proposition you right *out* of your uniform, and it has everything to do with who you are."

"How long's it been?" he groaned as they undressed each other in Sky's bedroom, "besides too long?"

"Three days," Sky whispered, making it sound like three months. When she'd dropped the last of his clothes on the chair, she sat on the bed and watched him. With agonizing slowness his gaze drifted from her eyes to her cheeks and across her breasts. She closed her eyes, damning the flush rising from her collarbone.

"Now who's blushing," Ryan murmured as he bent to trace the path of color with his mouth.

"Ryan, you're making me very self-conscious."

"Never that, Sky. It's one of the things that makes you so hard to resist. You're so confident, so completely unpredictable. When I realized it was you out there tonight, I thought, 'My God, she's walking to the station.'"

"Well, it has been three days. I thought somebody had put you in protective custody."

Ryan laughed. "No, the time just gets away from me. I mean to call, but you're asleep, and when you're awake, I'm asleep."

"We're both awake at the moment," she murmured.

Ryan's eyes darkened as he touched her and watched her breathing deepen. Her breasts rose and fell rapidly, and her desire built as she saw the change in him. It was a lovers' cycle, about to be perfected. She lay back, craving the heat he ignited, mindless as the flames engulfed her.

"Sky," he repeated until the sensual chant set a rhythm to her movements. "Yes," he whispered, his voice full of demand as she replayed his every caress over his tight body. Sleep was the furthest thing from their minds.

Sky rose early enough in the morning to dress, greet the painters and have coffee ready before they set to work in the stairwell. She settled in the library with a cup of coffee. She intended to measure the parlor windows for swags and jabots, the style of drapes she'd finally decided on, but instead she kept glancing through the doorway into the hall.

Fifteen minutes later she climbed the stairs with a breakfast tray. She eased open her bedroom door, expecting to find Ryan's dark hair peaking out from the duvet, but he was standing at the window, wrapped in a towel. He turned at her entrance.

"Good morning! I was just thinking about those pebbles I threw at this window when we were kids. Didn't I dare you to sneak out?"

She put the tray down on the bed. "You dared me, and said I didn't have the nerve with my parents across the hall. You'd parked the truck on Pilgrim Street."

He arched his eyebrows. "Total recall."

"Yup. I didn't get caught, you did. May I ask what you're doing in a towel?" she whispered with a quick glance at the door.

"Getting ready for a shower. Want to join me?" As he talked, he bent his knee and scooped up her skirt and slid his hand along her thigh. When Sky grabbed his shoulders to keep her balance, he laughed seductively. "A nooner, babe, I dare you!" The towel fell to the floor.

"Branigan, it's only breakfast time. Stop that!"

"Then we'll make it a niner," he said in her ear as he reached the elastic band on her underwear.

"There are three men right outside the door. You're insatiable, incorrigible and too fresh for your own good."

"You remembered."

"Ryan!"

"Coward," he laughed and picked up the towel. "The Janey Schuyler I remember loved insatiable, incorrigible and fresh."

Sky pointed her finger at him. "Yes, but she knew where to draw the line, even if her boyfriend didn't."

He slung the towel around his neck. "You don't know what you're missing."

"Do you know how many times I had to listen to that!" Sky whispered.

Ryan leaned against the doorframe to her bathroom and gave her a lidded look. "And was I right?"

She threw a pillow at him and left.

Once she was back in the kitchen, she thought about it. Under the banter it had seemed important that she turn him down. It was proof to herself that she still had some control over the emotions wrapping themselves around her. She wanted Ryan to see it as proof, too. He wanted fun and games, and so did she. Didn't she? They were so ridiculously mismatched in every other way, that that must be all she wanted. She enjoyed sitting by the hearth fire, sharing thoughts and plans—he was the proverbial "strong, silent" type, keeping everything inside. Sky dismissed the hollow feeling in her chest and looked out at the common.

She was back in the library when the shower stopped, and ten minutes later she watched as a uniformed police officer descended the stairs. "Good morning," he said brightly to three shocked painters. Each of them turned his head and watched him go into the library.

"I'm off, Sky," he said. "I should be out of this uniform, for one thing, and Kevin's gotten me to promise to help with the workshop."

"Fine," she said too brightly. "I'm up to my ears here, anyway. I may run into Boston for a few days...I have some things to order."

"Good. Give me a call when you get back."

A little regret in his voice would have been nice Sky thought.

There hadn't been any new snow, and what had fallen was finally beginning to melt. The highway was dry as Sky drove north, out of Plymouth County toward Boston. She drove the Mercedes through Boston's financial district and exited at Quincy Market at the bottom of the back side of Beacon Hill. The snow in the city was dirty slush. She maneuvered past the government buildings, up the hill and around to Mt. Vernon Street.

The house that her grandfather Greenleaf had bought in the thirties was a Bulfinch-designed colonial, solid brick with granite quoining and nearly priceless on today's market. Beyond its pure lines and prime location, it had what nearly every city house lacked, a driveway. Sky drove the Mercedes over the cobblestones and parked near the service entrance.

Sky hoped her taste in decorating was inherited, for she wanted to bring to Schuyler House the same beauty and sense of rightness that this house had. It was full of heirlooms, fine family pieces and portraits of museum quality, but it was homey, as well. It was part of the privileged world in which Sky had always moved, but because it was second nature to her, it involved no pretense.

She saw Ralph Shields during the afternoon and placed her order for the swags and matching slipper chair. He talked her into dinner at the Ritz and joked about her lack of concentration on the meal.

Sky laughed. "You're right, Ralph. I'm seeing someone in Millbrook, and I was just wondering if he'd ever let me drag him up here for dinner."

"Provincial?"

She smiled at the choice of words. "No. He just lives the way he wants. New Year's Eve was quite sophisticated, as a matter of fact. Do you know Santé?"

"Of course! It's a marvelous place."

The fact that Ralph's assessment cheered her up seemed childish. What did she care whether Ryan Branigan would dine at the Ritz?

Her second day in Boston, she combed Newbury and Charles Streets for andirons, as Schuyler House had four fireplaces on each floor. She found a pair of solid brass ones with a fender in a little shop on Beacon Street, close enough to be carried back up the hill. She went back to the Market for lunch and sipped a Dubonnet at Cricket's. Ryan would like this, she thought and then reprimanded herself for qualifying so much of her time and taste in terms of his.

The hour and a half drive back to Millbrook involved commuter traffic, and she got off the highway early, entering town by Duxbury Road. It was dark, and the snow was spotty under her headlights as she passed the bogs and the golf course. The bogs were newly sanded. The Branigans had been busy while she was gone. She found she liked coming home.

Sky made herself soup and a sandwich, which she ate in front of the television in the library. Gucci, Neiman Marcus and Lord and Taylor bags sat at her feet. At nine she pulled the phone into her lap and called Holly.

"Too late to call a pregnant person?" Sky asked after her friend's hello.

"Heavens, no! It's not the fatigue, it's the indigestion. Six weeks to go and I can't eat a thing. Never mind me, how are you?"

"Fine. I've been buying out Boston, and Ryan wanted me to give him a call when I got back. I didn't think I should make a personal call to the station, and as much as I like him, you're easier to talk to than Kevin."

"Kevin's a softy, just like the rest," Holly said. "He's afraid it'll ruin his image if it gets out. Anyway, Ryan's not working. His P.I. assignment's over."

Sky murmured a small "Oh?"

"Yes. He finished up last night. Why don't you call him at the house."

"I might," Sky replied. "Holly, was this a surprise?"

"I don't think so. I'm sure he knew because Drew worked out the sanding schedule with him. If he didn't mention it, he probably forgot. You know how busy he's been."

"I know."

"Sky?"

"Yes?"

"Call him," Holly repeated.

Ten

___

You're home!"

Sky put down the paste wax and adjusted the phone. "I know, Ryan."

"Well, I thought you'd call. It's Saturday afternoon, Foxy. Holly said you called her last night." His voice didn't sound annoyed.

"I thought you'd be at the station," she said.

"Nope, assignment is over," Ryan said.

"And I had to hear *that* from Holly." The silence hung between them as if Ryan found the need to assess the conversation.

"What does that have to do with us?" he asked finally.

It's part of you, she wanted to say, and *you* have to do with *me*. "Not much, I guess."

"Well, I'm glad you're back. I missed you."

It was the way he said it that made her sigh. "Thank you. I hope your brothers and those kids have kept you occupied."

"Yes, but they're no substitute for you. Nothing is."

Her voice caught, and she heard his sigh as they hung up. Twenty minutes later, as she was buffing the paste wax on the tea table in the parlor, there was a rap on the front door. She caught sight of Ryan through the windows by the door.

"This is a surprise," she said to him.

"I came to apologize in person." His eyes never left hers as he stepped into the foyer.

"For what?" She put the cloth on the table, which gave her an excuse to take her eyes from him. Far too much of something she was unprepared to think about increased her heartbeat.

"The Police League was given six tickets to tonight's Celtics game. I thought you were still up there... I gave the extra ticket to Kim. I'm taking them all into Boston in an hour and a half. I'm sorry." He touched her face affectionately.

She shrugged away the disappointment. "Kim will like it better than I would."

He nodded. "Maybe. I thought about stopping by and surprising you on Mt. Vernon Street, as a matter of fact."

"Then it's just as well," she said too quickly. "I wouldn't want those boys being given a tour of a Boston town house which is empty most of the time, anyway. I'd just as soon you didn't mention it, if you haven't already."

His expression grew guarded. "You sound just like my brother...."

She touched his jacket sleeve. "I didn't mean to offend you, but it's full of antiques which aren't mine.

Having the boys there would make them my responsibility."

"And God knows, you've never wanted any of that!" Ryan snapped.

His words stung. "Isn't that part of what makes me so appealing, Ryan? I don't want to be responsible for you any more than you want to be responsible for me. We're a matched set, Branigan, with separate lives *most* of the time. Don't criticize my values, and I won't criticize yours. I'm happy to spend time with Eric and his friends on your ground, but teenage delinquents don't belong in antique-filled houses. As a matter of fact, you should know that, too."

Ryan softened. "You're probably right. I don't take that stuff too seriously, and I didn't think it through—not that any of the boys would be a problem."

Sky relaxed, as well, and allowed herself to enjoy the pleasure she felt at being back in the same room with Ryan. "Whether anybody takes it seriously, it's still my responsibility."

"You're right." He smiled. "You smell clean and homey, even over the paint fumes."

"I've been waxing the furniture in the parlor. It's not finished, but the pieces have been moved back in. I ordered the draperies while I was in Boston. I see your eyes glazing over," she said with a laugh. "I won't bore you with any more details!"

Ryan put his hand over hers. "You never bore me, Sky. You make me breathless just trying to keep up. Sometimes it seems that everything in your life comes so effortlessly. Yet the thing is, where most women in your position would be sitting back taking it all for granted, you're running around all supercharged. I can't even be in the same room without feeling your energy." He pulled her into his arms and moved his hands across her back. "It makes me crazy. It always has."

"I don't mean to make you crazy," she managed to whisper as he kissed her. When he dropped his hands to her waist and followed her belt around to the front, she offered no resistance. "Then, again, there's nothing wrong with the level of energy you generate, Branigan."

Ryan made love to her where they were, on the wide leather couch with clothes scattered over the coffee table and easy chair. He was as affectionate as he was passionate, laughing and nuzzling with her long after they lay satiated. Sky could feel his contentment as he held her, reluctant to get back to reality. His happiness was real and she tried to ignore her frustration at not sharing more of his life.

"I hate to give this up," he murmured, caressing her hip.

"I hate for you to," she replied, but he was the one who finally reached for their clothing.

He left her at the front door with a lingering kiss, still apologizing for having to go to the basketball game. Still, she didn't want to go, and Ryan didn't need her along.

The following morning was gloomy. Millbrook closed in on itself under the oyster sky, low as a living room ceiling. What snow was left was old, shrunk to dingy frozen lumps along Main Street. Ryan called and asked if she'd like company. "Yes," Sky replied. "How about at your house? I'm tired of staging and drop cloths and the smell of turpentine."

"Really? I thought paint thinner ran in your veins," he replied.

A house with some Branigans in it guaranteed conversation, humor, and perhaps insight into Ryan's life. Sky didn't know what she hoped to gain, but what she stood to lose was more heavy breathing. It was clear to her that Ryan had settled into an affair he found completely satisfying, *as was*.

Sky called Holly and told her where she'd be, extending an invitation to drop by with Drew. "You might pass the word to Sean and Anne, too. If they're free, we can make this a party."

"Not likely," Holly replied. "Even though it's Sunday, if Sean's off, he'll be at the barn, I think."

Work, work, work, Sky thought as she backed her car out of her carriage barn, picked up the *Boston Globe* and *New York Times* at the deli across the street and drove out to the bogs. Holly had been right. Sky was greeted by women. Katey and Suzanne were stretched out with the dogs in the great room, and their mother and Holly were making lunch in the kitchen. "We did manage to talk the men into a lunch break," Anne said.

Sky went to the window. "Would I be in the way if I walked over?"

"I doubt it," Anne replied.

Sky put her parka back on and walked across the courtyard. The wide barn doors were closed, but the smaller door was open. The voices she could hear inside were deep and sharp. She stood in the doorway and saw Kevin on the ladder, and Sean standing by with a tape measure. "I don't want to be out here any more than you do," Kevin called down to Ryan. "If you were around during the week, we wouldn't have to be here at all."

"But I'm not," Ryan said.

"Something's going to crack, Ryan. Between the boys, the jobs and now Sky, you haven't got ten minutes," Drew snapped.

Sky saw Ryan turn around. "It's my life, damn it!"

"But what you do affects everybody else. You don't live out here in a vacuum," Drew continued. "It's about time you thought about it."

"Stop lecturing as if I'm Holly and you're out to change her mind. Of course I've thought about it. It's all I do sometimes. I've turned down the department up to my limit, Drew, what the hell else is left?"

"We're left," Kevin said, coming down the ladder. "We're left short-handed in the midst of the biggest expansion we've ever had. Your time is up, Ryan. If the town meeting approves the chief's request for another officer and you take it, I want to buy you out of the business."

"The hell you will," Ryan shot back.

"I can't afford the dead weight. I'll hire a partner to replace you, and you can concentrate on criminal justice. If it's what you really want, none of us will stand in your way, but you can't expect to have it both ways."

The accusation in Ryan's voice was unmistakable as he turned to Sean and Drew. "You've talked about this with him, haven't you? Sean, you're no different."

"I'm not a full partner any more than Matt and Jody are, Ryan. Besides that, I've been taking up the slack for you all year. It's one thing in January, but in the fall it's another story. I agree with Kevin and Drew. Treat this like the business it is. You're either in or out."

"Jerks!"

Sky had already turned to walk back toward the house. "Everybody's yelling at Ryan and Ryan's yelling right back. I think I ought to get going."

Holly shook her head. "They're brothers, Sky. Ryan was supposed to work yesterday till he got the Celtics tickets. The temper will disappear as quickly as it flared up."

Sky looked doubtful. "I don't think so this time. What has the chief got to do with it?"

"The police chief?" Anne asked. "The department is requesting another full-time officer. If Millbrook approves at the town meeting, the position will come up. Ryan has to put his name on the list as a P.I. He can only turn down the offer three times without having to give up police work completely. So *if* the position becomes available and *if* it's offered to Ryan, it's all or nothing this time."

"The pressure must be intense. No wonder they're at one another's throats."

Holly looked at Sky. "It's only because they want him in the business, and they need him more than ever."

"Except," Anne added seriously, "trying to force Ryan's hand won't work! It has never worked. He's a free spirit. None of the others ever were. I'm not sure Kevin understands Ryan's need to feel independent of all of them. It would be just like Ryan to accept the position out of spite, just so he can feel he's out from under. Up till this point, he's tried to make everybody happy. When he came back from Colorado, I think his brothers thought the restlessness had worked itself out, but I'm really not so sure. Holly, you haven't been around long enough to know how hard he's tried to give everybody what they want. Sky, you must see it in him."

Sky sighed and looked at the women. "Sometimes I think I don't know him at all. Our relationship is so compartmentalized. He doesn't share much of the stress, that's for sure. I like the strong part, but the silence is beginning to get to me."

They were interrupted by all four of the men as they came into the kitchen. A truce had been called, and the air between them was calm, if not cordial. They ate chowder and corn bread and a huge tossed salad Anne had brought with her. As much as Sky longed for Ryan to open up to her, she was pleased that the conversation never broached anything she'd overhead in the barn.

"Seems to me I invited you to dinner tonight," Ryan said to Sky as they finished lunch.

She arched her eyebrows. "Did you? I forgot. That was before I thought my house was being burglarized."

"It was before a lot of things," he whispered. "Are we still on?"

"Ryan, can you afford the time?"

He looked surprised. "Sunday night? Yes, I can afford the time."

When the brothers had gone back to the barn, Sky stayed long enough with Holly, Anne and the girls to relax again, and when Ryan picked her up at Schuyler House hours later, she was determined to get him to communicate.

They ate at a seafood place in Plymouth, far less formal than Santé, where the fishermen praised the chowder and the scrod was fresh. Ryan talked about the boys and the game and the goings on in Boston, and Sky reached over and took his hand as he drifted into reminiscing about his years in Colorado. The difference in Ryan was apparent by the time they finished the meal. He was relaxed, flirty, easygoing. When they'd finished and were back in his Bronco, he turned to look at her and rested his hand on her knee.

"Thanks, Sky, this was exactly what I needed. I'm up to my eyebrows in promises and commitments, trying to decide what to do with the rest of my life. I came down hard on you about lack of responsibility yesterday, but you were right: it's one of the things that draws me to you." He sighed and reached out to touch her.

"You're about the only person in my life who isn't demanding something from me. After a day of living up to other people's expectations, you're just what I need. I love the way you live; I always have, no strings, no pressure. You look at me with those big, honest eyes, and I know I satisfy something in you, too. Being with you still feels risky, Sky, like we're seventeen again. Risky and sexy and fun all over again." He started the ignition. "You're the only one in my overcrowded life who doesn't ask for more than I can give."

Sky knew he was implying that nothing more serious would work. She tried to convince herself that that was just what she wanted.

The pattern they'd established continued through the bone chilling January days and nights. A dinner invitation would be followed by a night of warmth and caring. Obligations would keep Ryan away for a while, and then he'd appear at the mudroom door.

If he waited too long, Sky would drive out to the barn and lend a hand with the construction project. When no one was looking her hand was just as likely to be found suddenly slipped into his hip pocket or she'd finger walk his shirt buttons. Just to heighten the suspense, she'd tell Ryan she was off to Boston for the day and then stay the night, or she'd plan to spend two days in the city and be back the same afternoon.

During an impromptu basketball game with Eric's crew, Ryan called *time out* only to swagger over to her spot in the bleachers and whisper deliciously suggestive ideas in her ear. There was no pattern to their days, no schedule for their time together. It made the passion unpredictable and they moved through those weeks in a constant state of anticipation, fun and games, as only two adults can play.

Ryan spent a week without a police assignment and put all his efforts into making amends with Kevin. That much Sky could see, though he still did little talking about his future in the cranberry business. The physical intimacy between them grew polished and perfect. They made love—though neither used the word—when and where they felt like it: in her shower with the painters below touching up the dining room ceiling, in the library after supper.

He gave her a complete tour of his own house, and after reminiscing over all the times she'd said *no* in the great room, Sky said *yes* in the front bedroom Ryan had taken over from Drew. Hadn't this been her heart's desire?

Toward the end of the month Sky spent three afternoons with Eric, Tony, Jason and Joe in order to be with Ryan. Kim, as always, was in attendance, too. Sky watched Eric's possessiveness, his casual jokes and quiet command of her. It was the antithesis of Sky's relationship with Ryan. The flashes of intellect and perception Sky had seen in Kim were rarely exposed when Eric was with her. "What's after graduation next year?" Sky asked her casually as they sat in the bleachers watching practice.

Kim shrugged. "Eric says marriage as soon as his uncle's garage in Plymouth works out steady. That's why he spends so much time working on cars. He's totally hot on engines."

Sky smiled. "So Ryan tells me. What about you Kim—is that what you want?"

The teenager blinked her lavender-coated lids. "Sure, why not?"

"I don't know—there are other things, other boys, other towns. There's life after the prom."

Kim laughed. "I like that, life after the prom."

"Well, there is; there are all kinds of jobs," Sky continued.

"You sound like my algebra teacher."

Sky looked at her. "You're taking algebra?"

Kim quieted. "Yeah, I kind of like math, and I do okay in it, so the guidance department talked to my parents."

"Have you thought about college?"

"Not really," Kim said, not sounding entirely convincing.

The scrimmage had broken up, and the boys jostled one another and Ryan as they came back to the bleachers and grabbed their gear. As they left for the locker room, Eric took the opportunity to give Kim a deep kiss. Kim resisted at first and then kissed him back as Eric's hand slid into the hip pocket of her jeans.

Four hours later Sky and Ryan sat in the library as she flipped through swatches of upholstery material for the Chippendale chair seats in the dining room. They were drinking Molson Ale from the bottle and nibbling crackers. "So, it's a toss-up between the blue-and-white bargello pattern and the brocade. Which do you think?" Sky said as she held up the samples.

"Either," Ryan replied without enthusiasm.

Sky sighed. "Look, I hung out at the gym all afternoon, and the least you can do is show a little gratitude by pretending you have an opinion."

"You should have gotten one from Holly."

"I'm not sitting on my couch, sharing my Canadian ale with Holly."

Ryan sighed, too. "Okay, okay, the bargello."

"You're sure?" Sky looked from one to the other.

"I'm sure. I really don't want to talk about chair seats." He got up and switched on the television.

Sky threw the swatches on the coffee table, knocking over the crackers. "Neither do I, Ryan, but what else is there to talk about? You never discuss *anything*!"

He turned around and faced her, his back to the set. "I'm sorry. I've got a lot on my mind, and I'm in a lousy mood. It's got nothing to do with you. I better go."

"Oh, no you don't, Ryan. I care about you, and that does have to do with me."

"Suit yourself." He finished the ale.

"The town meeting is on Monday night. That couldn't have anything to do with the tension, could it?"

He looked at her and then back at the television. "Maybe, I don't know."

"Well, hell, Branigan, there's nothing you can do until the chief's request comes before the voters, right?"

He nodded.

"So you won't even know whether you have a decision to make until the meeting, and even then you might not get called, right?"

"What are you getting at?" Ryan asked, turning around again.

"I've got the perfect solution to stress."

He sat back down next to her and munched a cracker. "Believe it or not Sky, I can't even get in the mood for that."

She scoffed. "Not sex, Branigan. Palm Beach."

Eleven

———

Sky turned and rubbed her hands along his shoulders, talking as she massaged his neck. "No heavy shirts, no sweaters, no snow, no worries. Let's take a few days and bake our brains. My tan could use some rejuvenation, and so could your entire system. Just you and me and the pool...moonlight...No brothers, no painters, no teenagers. We could leave first thing in the morning and be back Monday."

"The Schuyler way out" was Ryan's reply.

"What?" She dropped her hands.

"A little Palm Beach, a little sand and recreation, no reality, no responsibility. Life doesn't work that way for anyone but you, Sky. Just because I'm under pressure, I can't just up and leave."

She held back the frustration that was bordering on anger. "And what, may I ask, have I been for you all these weeks? Aren't I your version of Palm Beach, a little recreation, no reality?''

Ryan's face flushed, and his green eyes darkened. "And you've been complaining?"

They stared at each other. "Ryan Branigan, I'm no more to you than a means to relaxation, a rather nice way to release all that pent-up tension and anxiety; you said so yourself, and you thanked me for it! If I were out of your life tomorrow, you'd pick up the pieces in two days."

"Sky, you're being ridiculous. This is what you want, too. It's what you've always wanted."

"You're wrong," she countered. "I don't know what I want. Maybe I've never known, but the longer this goes on the more I know I want to stand on something firmer than quicksand."

"We have more than you think," Ryan added as she got up from the couch.

"That's not true!" Sky paced from the book-lined wall to the fireplace and back. "The most important decision in your career is staring you in the face, and the only people I talk about it with are Holly and Anne. Eric knows more about how you feel than I do. Which is exactly the way you want it...the way you've always wanted it."

"There doesn't seem to be much point in my staying" was the reply Ryan gave her, and when he left the house, she let him go. Let him stew in his own misery, she thought. He'd probably been tense and miserable since she'd first run into him, but she'd just been too star-struck to notice. Well, the euphoria was wearing off, and the place under her breastbone, so often overflowing with excitement and anticipation, felt hollow.

Sky went out for a walk at eight. There was little chance of a squad car stopping this time as she walked along the brick sidewalks, now free of snow. At the intersection of Main and Pilgrim, she turned right. Down the street, well-lit and welcoming, was the police station. She walked as far as the entrance and then backtracked. Once back at her own iron fence, Sky leaned against it and looked across the common to the fire house. She didn't know whether Sean was on duty or not. Sky went back into her house, which was bigger and emptier than that of anybody she knew in Millbrook. Ryan had been right, she thought: she *had* gotten everything she'd set out for in life, but this time it wasn't enough.

Southern New England has a weather phenomenon called the January thaw, and the temperature was heading toward the fifties when Sky awoke in the morning. It was the first time she'd dressed in a single layer in weeks. She pulled on a cotton turtleneck jersey and jeans to greet the painters, and while she was in the kitchen considering wallpaper samples, she caught sight of the Bronco across the common. As she watched, it left the fire station and came around into her driveway.

Ryan knocked at the mudroom door and entered without waiting. "I'm only here because I was in the neighborhood."

Sky gave him a sour look. "Take off your boots; you'll track mud all over the place."

"Does that mean come in?" Ryan was already unsnapping his vest.

Sky shrugged and closed the wallpaper book. "Might as well, since you *were* in the neighborhood."

She expected him to pull out a chair from the table or stoke the stove, but he walked across the room in his socks. The closer he came the more her heart pounded. "You're spoiled rotten, Janey Schuyler, you know that?"

"I'll thank you to keep your comments to yourself. There are men in the next room," she snapped.

Ryan sighed. "There are always men in the next room. At the snap of your fingers you call in experts to whip up thousands of dollars worth of restoration. If the color doesn't suit or the chair seat is wrong, you'll have them done over. There's not a silver platter big enough to hold what life has handed you!" She felt the stare and knew the set of his jaw.

"You're more beautiful than a woman has a right to be, more rich, more confident, more pampered. You live life on a whim, and when you couldn't deny the chemistry between us any longer, you decided I'd be part of that whim." Impulsively he grabbed her shoulders. "No matter what you said to me in your library, you like this relationship because it's fun, f-u-n, the stuff that runs your life."

"Hypocrite," she whispered back as she tried to follow her own advice and keep her voice down. "Fun is what *you* need, and now that you've got it, it's all you want. You're just like Eric and his attitude toward Kim. I'm something spectacular to hang on your arm or carry off to the sheets, and that, Ryan Branigan, is where your idea of a relationship starts and stops.

"I think you run yourself ragged on purpose so you can have the perfect excuse not to get emotionally involved." She poked his chest. "And *that* part of your life has been handed to you on a silver platter because you're just handsome and brash and desirable enough to get away with it." She was on a roll now, her eyes flashing, her face flushed. "I can't get you to talk about fabric or police work or cranberry harvesting, but the minute I swish a little hip I get your undivided attention."

She looked at his face and pointed her index finger at him. "Don't you dare laugh. You couldn't keep your hands off me for twenty-four hours. Admit it, Branigan, you're stuck with a terminal case of arrested puberty, characterized by hormone overdrive."

He grew cautious, and his laugh settled into a sly smile. "I've never enjoyed what wasn't freely given, Foxy."

"That's beside the point." She took a huge breath and put her hands on her hips. "I dare you to try. I dare you! Twenty-four hours together with nothing but conversation."

He looked intrigued. "And you? Am I that easy to resist?"

"Of course," she sniffed.

"What if I lose?"

"You have to bare your soul. You have to answer anything I ask honestly, openly, freely."

"A fate worse than death," he said soberly.

"I am *not* kidding."

Ryan leaned on the counter. "What if I win?"

"You won't," Sky replied too quickly. "Confidence is part of my scintillating personality, remember?"

"For the sake of tranquillity, I'll call it a long shot. On the off chance that I win, I want a deal out of you. If I win, I want you to let Tony and Eric and the others paint your pantry, and I want you to pay them to do it."

Sky stared at him so hard she could see his pupils contract. Neither of them blinked. "You're out of your mind," she whispered. "This is a national historic landmark, and the money you think I'm throwing around is to restore it for posterity. I'm paying a bloody fortune to have it done right, and I draw the line at a bunch of hoods—"

"Careful!"

"No!" Ryan's unruffled composure made her blood boil.

"Then the bet is off," he said calmly. "You expect a major concession from me, as if I'm the only one with faults. Could it be, Janey, that I'm the only man who has ever met you toe to toe, or in this case, eye to eye." He looked searchingly into her blue eyes, then laughing he moved close to speak into her ear. "Maybe in this case we're toe to toe, and eye to eye and—"

"Branigan," she gritted through her teeth, moving her head against her shoulder to avoid the inevitable goose-flesh, "choose something else."

"I have everything else," he whispered, and just as she was about to pull away, he went and poured himself a cup of coffee.

"I just don't want them ruining my house," she tried.

He looked at his mug. "Is that it? Or is it that you don't trust them in it? Afraid they'll leave with your silver spoons in their hip pockets?"

"Yes, damn it, and why shouldn't I be?"

"Because they don't deserve your distrust. They're poor and rough, and they haven't had a fair shake, but that doesn't make them thieves. People like you have been looking down their noses at them all their lives. You harvested our bogs with Jason's uncles, did you know that? This might be just as good for you as it would be for them." Ryan walked to the butler's pantry door and looked at the shelves and the cabinets. "You're a Schuyler, big bucks to those kids, and to them that means power, the kind of power their families have had to kow-tow to all their lives. They don't trust you any more than you trust them. A little one-on-one might make a world of difference.''

"I suppose that's why you've had them hanging around your house all this time, so you could impress the point on Kevin and Drew?'' Sky demanded.

"Astute observation.''

Sky sighed. "This all started as a joke. How on earth did we get so serious?''

"I don't know, but maybe it's about time,'' Ryan said, sipping the coffee.

"All right. You haven't got a prayer, anyway. I'm sorry I made such a big deal out of this. By the time I'm finished, you'll be jogging around the common in gym shorts, trying to cool off.'' She had come next to him, and while not an inch of him touched her, no more than a breath separated them.

"When do we start?'' Ryan asked.

She looked at the Rolex on her wrist. "Right now. I bet that you can't keep your hands off me until ten-o-two tomorrow. If you lose, you talk, and if I lose—and I won't—your overage urchins will paint the pantry.'' She put out her hand to shake his.

"Careful, you touch me, and we'll have to call the boys.''

Sky snorted and started from the room. "If you'll excuse me, I'm going upstairs to pack a few negligees. I suggest you call Kevin and square things before you leave.''

"Leave?'' Ryan snapped.

Sky brushed her hair through her fingers. "Didn't I mention that I have a two o'clock appointment with Ralph Sheilds on Newbury Street? I'm leaving in about fifteen minutes, and I can't see that this contest will be a fair one unless you come with me. Cheer up, it's not Palm Beach.''

Ryan's hand shot out to grab her, but she raised her arm. "Careful, Branigan, I'd hate to hear your deepest fears and fondest desires over brunch in the library.''

"You're playing with a stacked deck! And what was that crack about running around the common?''

She gave him her sweetest smile. "I better not comment on stacked decks, Ryan, love. I meant the Boston Common. It's just across Beacon Street.''

"You're not playing fair, Sky,'' Ryan said evenly.

"As long as I'm playing, isn't that what counts? As soon as I throw my things together, I'll drive over to the bogs and pick you up. You go on home now in the Bronco. Don't forget the jogging shorts.''

"I intend to enjoy this,'' Ryan muttered as he grabbed his vest and left the house. Sky was laughing out loud by the time she reached her bedroom. This was going to be more of a challenge than she'd had in ages, and the best part was that there was a lesson to be learned. Ryan wouldn't be able to resist the seduction she had in mind, and once he lost, she had every intention of introducing him to the joys of verbal communication.

Sky dressed for the city in a wool skirt and oversize sweater. It was warm enough to forgo her quilted coat, so she flung it in the back seat with her single piece of luggage. The only clue that she was up to something was the hint of makeup that freshened her faded tan.

Sky eased her car down the hill between Holly's Bittersweet Bogs and the Branigan's and spotted Ryan in the doorway of the barn. It was her last chance to openly admire him, and she took full advantage of it. He was in cords and a teal-blue sweater, a simple wool without weave or pattern, and instead of his usual down vest, he had on a tweedy sports jacket. The collar was up against the wind, and his hands were in his pockets, as if he hadn't a care in the world when he had so many. The depth of the affection Sky felt for him made her shake her head. She got out of the car and was pleased to note the change in his expression when he looked at the way she was dressed. It would have been nice to watch steam rise from his collar, but she made do with the way his voice caught when he said, "You look very nice."

"Thanks," she said. "All ready?"

"Sure," he replied, turning for her car.

Kevin came from the wall he was sheetrocking. "This is the damndest excuse he's used yet for getting out of work."

Sky felt herself flush and caught Ryan's look of delight. "You didn't think I could just skip town without squaring this with the boss, did you?" he asked innocently.

"He even asked if I cared to wager which way this little contest might fall," Kevin teased. "You turned him upside down when he was a kid. I expect you can do it again, if you haven't already."

"Just one minute," Ryan muttered.

Sky smiled at both of them. "On that note, shall we get going?" She handed the keys to Ryan. "You always loved to drive this car... be my guest."

"I am." He picked up a small bag from the rear bumper of the family truck and tossed it into the back with her things.

"That's it?" Sky asked.

"Change of underwear and my razor should just about do it," Ryan answered.

"No shirt and tie? What if I treat you to the Ritz?"

Ryan held the passenger door open for her. "You and I, my little fox, are dining alone tonight." His tone said everything, and as she sat in her seat, he unlocked the trunk and threw in an armful of logs and scrap from the barn. "Your fireplaces are in working order?"

Sky nodded.

"I thought so. What's a Boston Brahmin in her town house without a gently flickering fire, some good brandy and a red-blooded Irishman?"

It seemed to Sky that things might get a little tougher than she'd anticipated.

Twelve

Sky chose an innocuous radio station for background music as they left Millbrook and skirted Plymouth. She talked about Santé and the Carters and watched the sand hills give way to civilization. They picked up Route 3 and headed due north. The landscape was either brownish green and puddled or sprinkled with gray remnants of dirty snow. "We need a good healthy snow again," she said easily.

As they passed through Braintree and Quincy and headed toward the Boston skyline, Sky shifted in her seat and hiked her skirt slightly. "Excuse me," she said demurely. "I've got an itch."

Ryan kept his eyes on the road and the traffic.

She scratched and slid the fabric higher, and her hand disappeared long enough to capture his attention. When she'd settled back, she smiled.

"Panty hose problem?"

Sky turned to Ryan. "You silly man, I don't have a stitch on under this skirt."

Even in her seat belt she had to brace herself as the Mercedes swerved. The driver in the next lane gave an angry honk and raised his fist. Ryan's knuckles seemed a little white as he gripped the wheel. He looked at her from the corner of his eye, and when she smiled again, all sweetness and light, he put out his hand.

"Over so soon," she quipped only to have him yank it back.

"I can't believe I fell for that," he muttered.

"How do you know I was kidding?"

Ryan didn't reply. In fact he barely responded to any of her conversation as she talked about Jake and her mother and life in fashionable Florida. She mentioned how much she liked Holly and Drew and how cute Katey was; she was close to babbling. As they entered the city limits, she gave up and spoke only when she needed to give him directions.

They approached Mt. Vernon Street from the back of the hill, squeezing through the traffic, local and tourist, surrounding Quincy Market and Government Center. "How can you stand this?" he muttered. "I've got claustrophobia already."

The car inched past the now-fashionable brick row houses on the back of the hill, many of which had originally been carriage houses and servants' quarters for the grander homes on the other side. They came up Mt. Vernon at a crawl. "Right here," she said.

"My God, you've even got a driveway."

"Lucky," Sky replied.

He shrugged and killed the engine. "I don't know that luck had much to do with it."

Sky eyed him cautiously. The swing in their moods between flirting and pensive was giving her a headache. She got out of the car fighting the feeling that bringing him to Mt. Vernon Street had been a mistake.

Ryan took his time before they went in through the service entrance. He scanned the symmetry, looked at the shutters and the brick work. "It's my dream to make Schuyler House as inviting as this is," Sky told him when he finally joined her at the door. There wasn't a whole lot in his expression to indicate that he considered it inviting.

They entered through the kitchen, one built for utility and hired help. It had floor-to-ceiling cupboards with an industrial stove and the original porcelained cast-iron sink. She pulled open the refrigerator door.

"I suppose you had it stocked?" Ryan said over her shoulder.

"You did say we were dining alone at home?"

"I did."

Sky turned around. "Where is your brother living? Isn't Matt in Boston with the women I met New Year's Eve?"

"Marlborough Street, down between Gloucester and Fairfield."

At least it was conversation. "Would anybody be there this afternoon? You could go say hello while I'm at the decorators, unless you want to come along. Shields and Stone are right on Newbury, and I could walk over and join you..."

"I'll stay here. It's so inviting."

Sky sighed. "Ryan, you've never been the sarcastic type, and I don't think this is the time to start unless you're determined to lose the bet. Believe me, when you act like this the last thing on my mind is getting any closer than I already am."

"You're right. It was a cheap shot. I'm sorry."

The apology surprised her. "This is part of who I am, Ryan. It's about time you saw the house I grew up in." She sighed and picked up her overnight case. "I'm going to put this upstairs. Why don't you look around. The library is off the hall on the right—it's the most comfortable."

He followed her from the kitchen and gave quick furtive glances through the open doorways at the different rooms. When she came back from the second floor bedroom, she found Ryan, not in the study, but the formal front living room. He was looking at a full-length portrait of her that stood on the polished top of a China Trade campaign chest. She was in a sleeveless gown and kid gloves that covered the length of her arms, the white ensemble set off by her tan and the yellow gold of her hair cascading over her shoulders.

Ryan turned as she came into the room, his expression softer than it had been all day. "I thought it was your wedding picture," he said, "but that's the way you looked the last time I saw you."

"You're right. When I was a debutante, that was my coming-out portrait from Christmas."

"We were planets apart, even in Millbrook," Ryan replied.

Sky tried to concentrate on the fact that his declaration was in the past tense. "Only in some ways, Ryan," she responded.

He moved across the room and looked over the fireplace at an oil portrait of a mother and child. "You?"

"Yes. I'd like to bring it home with me one of these days."

"How old were you?"

"Six, I think. About the same age as you in the one of your mother and brothers that's in your family room."

Ryan nodded. "You and your mother. You know, I still don't think of you in terms of a family. You've always just been Sky. Maybe because I avoided your parents so much that summer."

Sky ran her hands over the back of a love seat facing the fireplace. "It wasn't so much that they disapproved of you. They just worried about how intense the whole thing was. I had such a crush on you, Ryan, that I would have walked on coals, if you'd asked me to."

He looked surprised. "No, Sky, you wouldn't have. It was the thing that held me all that time. I had girls calling me, hanging all over the place. You were the only one I ever had to chase. Even after—when you were gone, none of it seemed real."

"Well, I'm real, and so's the rest of the family. Life at the Schuylers wasn't the cozy chaos of the Branigans, that's for sure. We're independent of each other. We were brought up that way, and so were my parents before us. Off to school, off to camp—"

"Off to Europe, and now when you get bored, off to Palm Beach or off to Beacon Hill," Ryan finished.

Her concern for the mood returned. Whatever sexual tension and challenge had hung over them till now had dissipated. Ryan's concerns, melancholy, worry—whatever it was—threatened her. She wanted to shake it off or back away from the direction they were taking. Her dream and demand for conversation from this strong, silent man suddenly seemed a Pandora's box.

"Well," she said to break the silence, "now I'm only off to the refrigerator. How about some lunch?"

She made soup and sandwiches while Ryan set two places at the end of the dining room table. Ten friends could have joined them and not filled the space. He picked up his soup spoon and looked it over. "Stainless, a humble touch."

She looked at his guarded green eyes. "I think sterling is a little pretentious for a can of Campbell's, don't you?"

He put down the spoon. "We could have played this game in Millbrook. There's more to this than some stupid bet, isn't there?"

It was hard to keep her glance level, but she managed. "I can't remove myself from all of this any more than you can turn your back on the bogs."

"I may turn my back on the bogs, as a matter of fact. I did, you know, for years, and if I take on the police position—"

"Ryan, you came back from Colorado for one thing, and for another, I heard Kevin tell you that if you choose the police work, you have to sell your interest in the business. You'd cut off your arm first! I can see how much you care about the business *and* the job and your family, for that matter." She sighed and propped her elbow on the table. "Ryan, I can see all of it, but what I want so badly is to have you share it with me."

"It has nothing to do with you, Sky. I want that part of my life separate from what you and I have. It has to be." He got up from the table, and she followed him into the kitchen.

"Well, the first reason I dragged you up here was to be alone with you so you'd have to open up. But the second reason is because, unlike you, I want to share what I am."

"Great. Rubbing my face in it really makes me want to discuss my future in Millbrook."

"Ryan! None of this means anything," *without you*, she wanted to finish. The revelation shocked her. At that moment their entire relationship seemed to hang by a thread no stronger than spun sugar. They'd built themselves a gingerbread house from passion and desire on a foundation of fantasy. It hadn't occurred to her that Mt. Vernon Street would do this. Ryan stood like a stranger in her own kitchen.

"This means everything," he was saying. "This *is* you. You're right."

They communicated so beautifully physically, so why couldn't they verbally? "Let's go back tonight. I'll be finished with my appointment by four. We can pick up dinner in Plymouth on the way home," Sky blurted out.

Ryan just shrugged. "I don't intend to back down from this dare, Sky. You set me up, dragged me here, and I'll see it through. Go keep your rendezvous with the decorator. I'll be here when you get back."

Ten minutes later, she grabbed her purse and pulled on the coat. Ryan walked her to the front door. When she was out on the stoop, he called her name. "Sky?"

She turned around. "Yes?"

"Did you remember to put your underwear back on?"

It was the first hint of amusement she'd seen in his face in an hour. If these were the crumbs he was throwing to salvage the day, she might as well nibble. "Why, Ryan," she replied, "want to come out here and check for yourself, or would you rather just sit in this big empty house and stew about it while I'm gone?"

He gave her a look and a mutter, which she supposed was his way of letting her know he wanted things back the way they were. She didn't, but the alternative was too ominous. Ryan Branigan on his own terms was better than no Ryan Branigan at all.

She left the hill with a small sense of relief and a huge feeling of frustration, which she squelched concentrating on the tasks at hand. She met with Ralph and ordered the bargello for the dining room chairs and a companion fabric for balloon shades. When she'd finished, she took a roundabout route home. She'd wanted to walk to get a chance to enjoy the city. The wind was harsh as it blew off the Charles River, and she jammed her hands into her coat pockets as she crossed Back Bay. She took Gloucester Street from Newbury, gritted her teeth as she crossed the mall on Commonwealth Avenue and then began to look around when she reached the corner of Marlborough Street.

A right turn took her up the block between Gloucester and Fairfield. Matthew Branigan rented an apartment somewhere here. He probably talked his head off to Erin and Nancy. Drew, no doubt, told Holly his deepest secrets, and Kevin certainly let the world know what was bothering him. She left Fairfield and approached Exeter. Ryan kept acting as though she were expecting too much, but he gave so little. It couldn't possibly be all there was. She should have asked Holly how much he'd communicated with the banker, Johanna. Sky crossed Clarendon and then Berkeley. Obviously that hadn't been enough, either. You stubborn, stubborn man, she cried to herself. I can't help it if I'm rich any more than I can help loving you. That stopped her dead in her tracks at the corner of Charles and Beacon. That was it, wasn't it. Nobody got this irritated and pensive and moody and wary unless they were in love. Unless they were in love, and they didn't want to be.... Ryan most certainly didn't want to be. Did she?

She hurried along Charles, but instead of turning right up Mt. Vernon Street she headed past the shops and killed another hour by picking up reproduction mirrored sconces at Period Furniture Hardware. The sun was long gone behind the low brick buildings, and by the time she went back up to her grandmother's house, Beacon Hill was aglow with gaslight and parlor lamps.

Her own house was dimly lit. She let herself into the kitchen, and her nostrils flared at the aroma of roasting chicken. Just to make sure, she pulled open the oven door and found a foil-covered pan gently hissing with potatoes baking on the side. It made her smile.

"Ryan?" she called as she took off her coat and left it with the purchases in the hall closet. The strains of a symphony floated from the library. "I see you know your way around the kitchen."

"Growing up with a house full of bachelors will do that to you," he called from the front room. He sounded decidedly more cheery than when she'd left. "I've found my way around your stereo system, too. Sky, I poured you a bourbon, so come on in the library and join me."

Sky smiled. It was impossible to keep from being moved by the warm sound of his voice. "No, thanks," she called with a laugh. Nevertheless, she went down the hall. "You can't ply me with liquor tonight. That's the oldest trick—" She stopped short of the doorway when she realized that the low light coming from the room was flickering. One more step, and she was bathed in firelight. "What've you done?"

Ryan was sitting close to the fireplace in a high-backed Queen Anne side chair. At least that's where his voice was coming from. In the shadows she caught sight only of an amber liquid in an old-fashioned glass. "Nothing, babe," Ryan replied over the strains of Haydn. "I just chased the

chill a little with the logs in the trunk. You do remember
the logs?"

"Ryan?"

"Come in, Sky, and sit down."

"I don't think so."

"Can't trust yourself, huh? I knew it. I left your drink
at the cabinet."

It was as if nothing but goading and flirting had passed
between them all day. Sky didn't know whether to be irritated or grateful.

For lack of anything else to do, she crossed the room,
and picked up the drink and added ice from the silver
bucket. He was playing host to the hilt. The bourbon hit
her empty stomach like hot coals. She sipped again as it
began to radiate and dull the edge of her temper. Everything in the room was either bathed in shadows or re-
flecting the gold of the fire. "You don't think a shot of
bourbon's going to seduce me, do you?"

"No, but I might."

"You know what I meant," she continued, now having the courage to march around the chair and face him
squarely. She had her best smirk on her face, but the
expression froze. Ryan raised his glass in a toast. With the
exception of the oxford shirt he'd had on under his
sweater, he was dressed only in firelight.

Thirteen

Sky's laugh slid into a moan, and she put her free hand over her eyes. "What do you think you're doing?"

"Waiting for you, Sky," he whispered. "It seemed like hours."

The words hit her ears the way the bourbon had hit her stomach. She took another sip. "This isn't fair!"

He probably arched his eyebrows, but she wasn't looking. "We're not playing fair, remember?"

"Ryan," she moaned.

"Sky, do you know what you do to me when you say my name?"

Whether he was kidding or not, his chest rose and fell deeply. His fingers curled easily around the glass, and when he stretched his legs, she closed her eyes. His soft laugh made her swear. Whether she couldn't move or didn't want to was immaterial. When she opened her eyes, it was to find him looking at her. Ryan held her spirit in his hands, and the fear that he'd tear it to shreds with his complacency stabbed at her racing heart. The game they played was of her making, and he had only been following where she'd led. But now Ryan, the master of the ridiculously seductive scene, insured the return of fun and games.

She hid the pain. The only perfect thing between them was this, and now it was just a smoke screen to keep both of them from what they'd come so close to facing hours earlier. The light licked and flickered over Ryan, and he put down the glass to begin unbuttoning his shirt.

"Don't do that," she croaked.

He smiled. "I'd rather you did, now that you mention it."

She made a half turn. "I'll check the chicken."

"The chicken's fine," he declared. His gaze bore into her as she crossed the room.

"Well, I'm not," she snapped.

Ryan stood up abruptly, and she jumped back. "Yes, you are," he whispered. "You know you are. Nobody plays this the way you do."

They held each other's glance. "I don't want to play."

"You'd prefer conversation? You'd still have to win to get that out of me."

Sky finished her drink and put the empty glass on the blotter of the mahogany desk. Her choices were few. They were still eye-to-eye, and the desire in his was unmaskable.

She leaned against the desk and crossed her dress boots at the ankle. "I dare you to try and get these clothes off without touching me. Face it, Branigan, you've met your match."

The smile of delight deepened, and he set his glass next to hers. As she picked it up to take a sip of what he'd barely touched, he began to unzip one boot. "I wouldn't drink that if I were you."

Sky cocked her head. "Think I've had enough?" She put it to her lips and made a face. "This is tea!" The boot came off with a gentle tug. "Ryan, you cheated!"

"Give me your other leg." She didn't need to because the long, thin zipper was already being maneuvered down her calf, and the kid leather fell open from knee to ankle. "Strategy is everything in this battle, Janey. A little liquor in you and a little tea in me." Her skirt fell in a wool puddle over the boots.

"How'd you do that?"

"Practice," he said. Somehow he'd gotten a grip on the hem of her sweater, and the next thing she knew, it was over her head. Ryan stopped then and stepped back. She was down to a camisole and half slip, and his breathing was decidedly less even than when she'd first stepped into the room. He picked up a silver letter opener from the desk and slid it under the strap on her shoulder.

A log fell into the embers and sent a hiss from the fireplace. The handle under Ryan's fingertips glowed as he moved his hand. The satiny fabric slid over the soft slope of her breasts, caught on the tips and drifted to her waist. Sky watched the agony of self-denial settle on his features, but nothing was as wrenching as what she was feeling.

"You're torturing yourself, Branigan; all you have to do is put your hand out. I'm right here."

He brought his head up and looked at her and began to unbutton his shirt, but the moment it was off, he turned and stepped to the fireplace. He took a deep breath and held it as the light played over him as if he were marble. Sky stepped next to him, her own breathing quick and uneven so that her breasts rose and fell. Ryan seemed mesmerized by it. He shook his head. "The game's over, isn't it?"

Something inside of her began to tear. "I'm right here, Ryan."

"You think you're in love with me, Sky. I've seen it coming. You're not, of course, any more than I'm in love with you, but I get the crazy feeling that you set this up to win so I'd pour out my heart. This *is* my heart, Sky. This much of us is perfect together, but the rest would be disaster. I care about you—you know that—but you've got no more business with a cop than I do in this house."

"Is that what you think?"

He nodded. "I thought about it all afternoon. I don't want to hurt you any more than I want to be hurt. If the scales are tipped, then we should quit."

Ryan had said too much already and she arched her back until the wonderful warmth of his fingers began their magic, almost erasing the pain of his words. "Truce," she whispered kneeling with him onto the carpet. When he'd settled onto his back, he raised his hands to her and Sky leaned over. She looked into the shadowed face of the man who'd just told her he didn't love her, that the very idea of it was impossible. He smiled and closed his eyes and she ached the way she had when they'd parted as teenagers.

Afraid that he might say more, she pressed her fingertips against his lips to hold back the hurt and leaned until her throaty whisper was at his ear. "Oh, Ryan" was all she was able to say.

He didn't speak again, even when she moved her hand from his mouth and caressed the familiar planes of his body. Instead he cupped her breasts and sucked the tender tips to hardened nubs as her exploration intensified.

A moan caught in his throat as he moved against her, locking her in an embrace. He opened his hands across her shoulder blades and kneaded his way down her spine until she was stretched over the length of him, breathing as he was in quick, shallow gasps.

He moaned again urgently until her desire to satisfy him began a whirlpool of sensations in her own body, deepened beyond her control as he moved his hands to guide his entry. In the midst of the sweet, rhythmic ecstasy, she felt Ryan shudder and tighten his embrace, prolonging the pleasure, wrapping her in melancholy. Actions speak louder than words, she thought as he shifted beneath her and they came back to reality.

When they finally began to stir from where they'd settled on the rug in front of the fire, Ryan handed her her clothes. "The boys will do a great job for you; there's no need to worry."

She came up on one elbow. "This was a truce. Your little band of painters wasn't part of a draw! It's not that I haven't been cooperative: I let them tinker with my car."

"Ask me anything, I'll keep my end of the bargain."

"You've said enough already," she snapped. Ryan was quiet, and when Sky realized he was watching her, she moved and began to dress. She threw him his shirt.

"They are going to spend the rest of their lives slamming up against people like you," he continued. "Men and women so removed from the real world that they wouldn't think to give a kid like Eric a chance. You don't want to know what I'm thinking any more, Sky, but the truth is you just breeze along living your perfect little life, scooping up people as if they were trinkets. You could use this as much as they."

"A good healthy dose of reality and responsibility?" she shot back.

"Yes, as a matter of fact. It might give you another goal in life besides decorating your house."

She busied herself pulling the sweater back over her head. "You really see me as the spoiled little debutante living on whims, don't you?"

Ryan pulled the rest of his clothes from under the chair. "It's part of your charm, I don't deny that. Being part of your whims is pure adrenaline."

"As long as the scales don't get tipped," she added.

"Be honest with yourself, Sky. When the house is finished, or you get fed up with the snow or my long hours, you'll be gone, out of my life just like before. Babe, even when I hold you, I can feel you pulling away. My God, I thought I'd die from wanting you, but I'm realistic enough to enjoy the attention while it lasts and let it go at that. I was worried that you thought you had to be in love with me to justify all of this."

Sky sat up. "I don't have to justify anything, but I'll be damned if I'm going to sit by and let you consider me shallow and prejudiced and narrow-minded. The boys can start tomorrow, and I'll pay top dollar." She gave him a long hard look. "If anyone is in love and can't stand to admit it, it's you. Now get up and come eat that chicken."

Half an hour later they were back at their places in the dining room with the chicken, vegetables and a bottle of Montrachet from the Greenleaf wine cellar. Sky pushed the peas around on the Wedgewood plate, trying to pretend she had an appetite. "The town meeting is tomorrow night," she said.

Ryan nodded. "The Finance Committee recommends approval of the chief's request for personnel, by the way."

"And that will be you," Sky said.

He shook his head. "Not necessarily, but I'm at the top of those who qualified. If it goes through, the chief will call for the list, and I'll have fourteen days to put my name on."

"So Kevin is pulling on one arm, and the police chief is pulling on the other. How serious are your brothers about wanting you to give up your interest if you aren't working actively?" Sky asked.

"Very. It would put me in the same category as Jody and Matt, who own about fifteen per cent."

"And what about family, Ryan? Do you get along well enough with Drew and Kevin to work with them day in and day out?"

Ryan watched her from across the table. "Interesting way to put it. I'd do anything for my brothers, and I've proved it more than once."

"To your satisfaction or theirs?" Sky asked, playing the devil's advocate.

"Both," he muttered. "I gave more than part-time, even when I was on call at the station. It's all been fine with me, just as it was."

"It doesn't seem to have done much for your social life," Sky threw in lightly.

Ryan looked at her over the rim of the wineglass. "There have been a few willing to take me as I am."

"That desperate for you, huh?" She smiled when he arched his eyebrows. "I suppose your banker friend that Holly mentioned asked too much. Probably thought somebody thirty years old might want to settle down, invest in some emotional security."

"We had emotional security just the way things were," Ryan replied flatly.

"Apparently not, Branigan."

"While we're on the subject, Sky, how about discussing your track record?"

She shrugged and finished her wine. "You know me. Footloose and fancy-free. No strings," she quipped, avoiding the green eyes.

"No children," Ryan added.

"Nope." Sky got up from the table abruptly and began to clear it. When Ryan came through the swinging door with the platter, she was scraping the plates. "I want to go home tonight," she said.

"To Millbrook?"

"Yes. You can bring Eric and Tony and the others over in the morning."

At nine o'clock that night, she drove Ryan up to his door. The corner of the barn and the rafters of the house had their floodlights on, catching the snow that had just begun to fall in beams of light. Smoke curled from the chimney, and through the window she could see Kevin adding a log to the wood stove.

Ryan grabbed his bag and got out, ducking to look at her from the open door. "It was a truce, wasn't it?"

"It was a stupid idea," Sky replied.

"Janey, there's no sense in digging unless you expect to get a little dirty. Play it as it lays, and don't get hit with any surprises. I thought that was your philosophy."

"It is," she answered too quickly. "Always has been. Now go feed your dogs or something. I'll see you in the morning."

The moment Ryan slammed the door, Sky shifted into gear and skidded over an icy patch. She swore once at the ice and once at herself as she drove up and out into town.

Since Sky's painters didn't work on weekends, there was little chance of annoying them with the unpleasant surprise that a handful of teenagers were going to tackle the pantry. With any luck at all, they'd finish up and be long gone by Monday morning. The boys arrived with Kim in tow, looking none too pleased and annoyingly curious. "Some digs," Eric said. "Totally outrageous."

"Thank you, I think," Sky replied with a look at Kim. "I'm glad you're here to translate."

Ryan started the band moving by having them stack everything in the dining room, and while they got to work, Kim wandered into the kitchen and found Sky. "They're really jacked about being here," she said, pulling invisible lint from her oversize black sweatshirt.

Sky smiled. "You seem a little down, though."

"Nah" was all she offered.

Ryan borrowed drop cloths from the professionals and set up his charges. "Everything is clean and ready to go. Don't screw up on me guys—this lady can give expert references."

From the safe distance of the kitchen, Sky watched Ryan as he put his arm around Jason while explaining something, then demonstrated the brush cleaning to Tony. In a way she supposed they were family, too, lost boys as he had been, not quite sons and not quite brothers. The lump in her chest was making its way to her throat.

Kim asked for the bathroom, and when she'd gone off, Ryan came into the kitchen. "They're off to a great start; I'll be back in a few hours."

"You're not leaving them with me!"

Ryan grinned. "They're harmless. Just crack the whip when it's needed. I promised Kevin." He glanced toward the mudroom. "It's Kim who gets in the way. Eric is in way over his head, I think, and she's really holding him back."

Sky's temper flared. "Eric spends the majority of his time making passes at her, Ryan. Don't you dare blame Kim. She's probably gotten him through school single-handedly."

Ryan's eyes widened. "Testy!"

"Maybe. Frankly I'm a little fed up with your infantile attitude about women and their roles in men's lives."

"Any women in particular?"

"As a matter of fact, with your track record, I'd say it applies to all of them. The more I get to know you the more obvious it is that your concept of an ideal relationship is one that takes place between two sheets."

Ryan responded with a lingering look somewhere between amusement and annoyance, however, Kim returned just then and they dropped the subject.

"Kevin's waiting," Ryan said by way of a goodbye, and Sky mumbled something as he turned to leave.

Tony and Eric worked diligently, and their skill was far from amateurish. After Kim had finished a third cigarette, Sky offered her a piece of coffee cake. "Put something in your mouth besides a filter," Sky joked.

"It's my life," Kim muttered.

Sky studied her. "Are you all right?"

"Sure."

"You're awfully quiet."

"I said I was okay," Kim snapped.

When Ryan returned after lunch, the first coat was finished, and the room smelled of paint and spaghetti sauce. Kim was stirring the pot, a fourth cigarette in her mouth. "Give it up while it's easy," Ryan said.

Kim jammed the butt into the sink drain. "Get off my case, will you?" she cried and left for the bathroom.

"See what I mean?" Ryan said under his breath to Sky. "A lovers' spat, and she's a pain in the neck. Hormones!"

Sky took over at the sauce pot. "I wish you wouldn't be so hard on her."

He acquiesced. "Sorry. Could I interest you in dinner at the house? Kevin is being wined and dined by his New Year's Eve friend, and the dogs have promised to behave."

His New Year's Eve friend, even that irritated Sky. "Does she have a name?"

"Who?"

"Never mind. No, I don't think so, not tonight." She wanted to tell him that something felt wrong. They were out of sync, and warmth was fading. It seemed dangerous to accept in her frame of mind, so she declined, and for the first time, Sky didn't even make a counteroffer.

"Suit yourself," Ryan said, turning to the pantry. "What do you say, guys—pizza on me tonight to celebrate?"

Fourteen

Sunday morning at ten, Kim, Eric and Tony arrived at the door, with the Bronco pulling away from the curb. "The boss is in a hurry," Eric said, "He's gotta get back to the barn. He'll be over later."

Sky watched the vehicle go around the common and closed the door. It looked like snow again. While the boys cleaned off years of paint from what had turned out to be solid brass drawer pulls and hinges, Sky led Kim into the library. "You seemed interested in the Branigan's collection. You're welcome to browse here and borrow some, if you like."

"You read a lot, I guess." Kim looked at the spines and their titles, then picked up a framed picture. "Florida?"

"Yes. That's my brother Jake and me with my father. He died about ten years ago."

"That's tough," Kim replied. "*Tom Sawyer*, we read that in English."

Sky sat in the easy chair. "What'll you do after graduation?"

Kim looked annoyed and flopped into the chesterfield. "My parents want me to go to the community college. I'll probably be married."

"Oh, Kim," Sky sighed. "It's so soon. You and Eric have the rest of your lives." She hated sounding like the adult she was. *It's so wrong,* she wanted to add.

Kim gave her a sharp look. "It's my life."

"Of course, but in a few years you could both change, and even if you didn't, you'd still be that much better for the time you waited."

"Geez! You sound just like my parents and their massive attitude problem. I've got more than Eric!"

Sky stood up. "Kim, I'm sorry, I didn't mean to get so personal."

Kim shrugged. "What do you think? I'm pregnant."

A bell sounded in Sky's head that turned the ache she'd carried around for two days into a jolt of pain. She managed to keep back the gasp and hold in the sorrow. "Are you sure?"

"I'm a week late; I'm never late."

"Does Eric know?"

"Sure."

"And your parents?"

"No way!"

Sky chose her words carefully as Kim lit a cigarette. "Do you mind if I ask if you've seen a doctor? Were you using birth control?"

The teenager bit her lip between long drags and exhalations. "Look, Jane or Sky or whatever I'm supposed to call you, I don't need any more adults breathing down my neck, okay? It's not your problem." She choked on the last of her words and blinked hard, all the while looking up at the highest row of leather-bound first editions. "Damn," she whispered as a tear finally worked its way through the mascara, taking some of it along as it slid over her cheek.

Sky grabbed a cocktail napkin from the bar and sat down next to her, aching to hold her but only offering the paper. Kim took it and wiped the smears along her lower lashes. "My parents'll kick me out. They hate Eric."

"But they love you. They'll need to know, if it's true." My Lord, she thought as she listened to herself, how easy it was to play advisor when the panic wasn't her own.

"I can't tell them unless I'm already married. They'd never let me keep the baby. Eric'll stick with me. I'm the best thing that ever happened to him." She smiled weakly.

"Do you want the baby? Do you think you can handle it?"

"No. Yes! Yes, of course, why couldn't I? What kind of a person do you think I am?" She was fighting sobs as her chest heaved, and she leaned against Sky.

"I think you're a bright person, Kim. One with a wonderful future who might be scared and confused. There's nothing wrong with admitting that you're too young to keep a child or that marrying at eighteen is too early." Sky stroked Kim's hair as she fought her own ache. "Would you like me to talk with your parents? I'll make a doctor's appointment and go with you. You don't have to go through this yourself. There are counseling programs right in Plymouth, people who can help, Kim."

The teenager leaned away from Sky and sat up. She dabbed her eyes with the remains of the napkin. "Why you? I don't mean anything to you."

"Yes you do, Kim. I care what happens to you because I like you, and I know how frightening this is. It happened to me."

Kim looked at Sky and blew her nose. "You? What'd you do?"

"It turned out that I wasn't pregnant, just very, very late and very scared. But if I had been pregnant and I'd married the boy, it would have been a disaster for all three of us. We were far too young and far too different to make it work. I still think about it today, and believe me, it was the last time I ever took a chance." Sky sighed and touched Kim's arm. "What we need to do is take this one day at a time. First we make sure you have something to worry about, okay?" When Kim didn't answer, Sky hugged her. "You can trust me; I hope you know that." When Kim finally nodded, Sky said, "Why don't you go upstairs to the first bedroom on the left? I've got lots of makeup in the dressing table and you can repair the damage in my bathroom."

Kim's smile was weak, but sincere. "Thanks. You're really awesome sometimes, Sky."

By the time Ryan returned at three, the pantry was finished, the hardware gleamed, Kim was composed, and the whole place was ripe with the smell of paint thinner and turpentine. "I admit I had my doubts," Sky said to Eric and Tony, "but you did a good job. If you're not too busy around spring break, you might consider giving me an estimate for sanding and painting all the exterior shutters and the trim on the carriage barn."

She ignored the look of surprise on Ryan's face and shook their hands before she wrote the check. As she closed the ledger, Eric gave Kim a hug and his hand opened at her belt line. Kim slapped it away and went for her coat. Ryan hustled them all out and held Sky's hand longer than necessary as he shook it. Other than that, there was little between them.

She watched at the door and then closed it against the bitter cold. The brief thaw had passed, and winter was back. The affair is over, she thought, killed on Mt. Vernon Street by the conversation she thought would save it. It would be just like a Branigan to be perfectly content to continue, but the relationship was growing more hollow by the night, a hollowness she felt in her heart.

As Sky snapped on lamps and thought about Sunday supper, Holly called. She talked about her rapidly approaching due date, the progress in the barn and Drew. Her recalcitrant brother-in-law was never mentioned, and Sky wasn't about to ruin the mood.

When the brass knocker thudded against the front door, Sky excused herself and hung up. Ryan stood on the stoop. Snow was melting in his hair, and he smelled of the Chinese food he was carrying. "My treat," he said.

She looked beyond him. "It's snowing."

"Yes, it is. Are you considering leaving me out here in the cold?"

"Not as long as you've got the egg rolls."

They spread the dinner on the coffee table in the library and spooned the boxed contents onto dinner plates. "I wanted to thank you," Ryan said.

"They did a good job, and I wouldn't mind hiring them again. You were right, Ryan," Sky answered.

"Was I?"

"About their talent, yes. For that I'm sorry. They deserve a chance, and I'm glad I'm in a position to give it to them."

Ryan ate and then looked at her. "And what about your talent, Sky? You keep insisting you're here for good."

"And I need a job to prove it? It's going to take half a year to finish Schuyler House, and for now, that is what I'm doing. I'm sorry if that bothers you. I waited for this for a long time, and it wasn't an easy decision, as a matter of fact. I came back essentially to nothing, not even friends. You were a happy accident. I don't need to work for a salary, and Schuyler House is my job. It's where my heart is."

"And when it's finished?"

"Ryan, I'll worry about that when the time comes. One day at a time, please."

"As always," he replied.

"Yes—and that's what you loved about this little fling of ours, or am I mistaken?"

He stabbed at his egg roll.

"I want to ask you something," she blurted out, "and I want a honest answer. *If* you'd been right, and I'd fallen in love with you—say that was my big confession while we were in Boston—would you be here right now, dinner in hand?"

His expression was guarded. "I would have wanted to be."

"That doesn't answer my question," Sky said.

He sighed. "Sky, there's been enough pain in my life. I don't want any more, and I don't want to be the cause of any. You're not in love with me—you said so yourself—so the point's moot, anyway. If we weren't on equal footing, no, I wouldn't keep seeing you."

The phone rang, bringing the revelation to an abrupt halt. Sky's hello was met with a sob and someone fighting for composure.

"Sky? It's Kim" came the tremulous voice. It broke again, this time into furtive laughter. "I got it. Oh, geez, I can't believe it!" She began to cry and laugh and hiccup. "I got my period; I'm not pregnant. Oh, Sky, I can't believe it!"

Sky's voice caught, and tears sprang to her eyes. "Wonderful. Let's keep the appointment, okay? Will you come over after school tomorrow so we can talk about it?"

"God, yeah, anything!"

"Okay, I'll be waiting. Get a good night's rest, I bet you haven't had one in a while."

Kim laughed. "You're right, thanks. I'm gonna call Eric."

"You haven't told him?" Sky said.

"Not yet. You were the first one I thought of."

Sky hung up and stared at the bookcase. "Kim?" Ryan asked. "She's something else. Eric told me yesterday that she thinks she's pregnant and wants to get married. It'll be the end of him; a wife and baby would sink him like a stone. She just dug in those claws and hung on—"

Sky's eyes had opened wide as he talked. "Is that what you think, that Kim's looking for a husband?" She stood up and bumped the table in her hurry to cross the room. "Men! You know nothing about it, nothing! Eric has been pushing her all along, but even that's beside the point. It doesn't matter who said yes: it's done. You'll never know the fear, Ryan. It's cold and clammy, and when you're a kid yourself, it closes in like a lid because nobody else can help. The people you love the most are the ones you can't bear to tell." She pointed to the phone, and her voice shook. "Kim called to tell me she's *not* pregnant, but for every Kim there are thousands of teenagers who *are* because some boy made them think sex was the greatest thing in the world." She realized tears were running down her cheeks. "You'll never know, Ryan, because for every girl who says no, dozens are in the wings, willing to take up the slack."

Ryan got to his feet so quickly that she backed up against the bookshelves. "You're talking about yourself! Sky, did you get pregnant that summer?"

She shook her head. "I went through exactly what Kim did. I thought I was, and every agonizing day in Europe I stewed and prayed and made myself sick with fear. It's a terrible lesson to learn."

He touched her shoulders. "You never told me. You never said a word. I asked, didn't I?"

"Asked! With Diana Middleton draped on the pool fence waiting for you. Never mind, Ryan, it was a long time ago. We were stupid kids who thought we could beat the odds." Her expression was so full of regret that his face fell. "The problem is, Branigan, I don't like myself very much like this. Kim and I will be fine, but you and I—" She stopped and moved away from his touch.

"You call the shots. You're the only one who could ever do that, you know. We're Kim and Eric in grown up bodies, and I hate it. There's no responsibility, there's no depth. Nothing! I don't love you—how could I when you won't let me? What you and I have should be the culmination of a relationship, not the basis for it. What if I got pregnant? We don't have any more foundation for raising a child or being a family than we did back then. I think it says something pretty shallow about both of us."

Ryan's green eyes darkened, and he closed them for a moment. "Whatever you and I set out to prove this time around is all proven, isn't it?"

"Yes, Ryan. You're still capable of seducing the rich kid from Boston. I can still pull the best-looking boy I ever knew from his work and his brothers."

Ryan reached for his parka and left the remnants of dinner where they were. "You were the only one who ever gave me a run for my money, Janey."

"So were you, Branigan."

His work boots left footprints over the aged brick walk, powdery with the new snow.

Sky chose not to attend the town meeting on Monday night and sat at home feeling like a bad citizen. Next time her voice would be heard and her vote counted. She just didn't want to sit huddled in the auditorium of Mill-brook High School, avoiding Ryan and his brothers.

Kim kept her promise, and the two of them spent long hours talking about the facts of life, responsibility and the future. It gave Sky's days a new focus and during the first week without Ryan, an emotional substitute. In addition, every hour Kim spent at Schuyler House was one less than she spent with Eric.

The *Plymouth Patriot* carried news of the town meeting, including the approval of the police chief's budget. Sky ached as she read it, unable to think of anyone who'd make a better cop. Ryan had the right combination of compassion and distance—the very traits that drove her crazy made him ideal for the position. His brothers recognized it too, no doubt.

Ryan, Ryan, Ryan. She sat and thought about him over a solitary drink. Independent, feisty, private... Why not, he'd coped with the loss of his parents at twelve, fought for his place between five other siblings, accepted an unorthodox homelife, put himself through school, turned his back on all of it and then came home. Something in Ryan had brought him back, settled him down and made him determined to reach out to anybody else he felt deserved better than what life was dish-ing out. She loved him for it, and that unpleasant thought made her bolt the last of the drink.

On Saturday Holly called and offered Sky her tickets for the evening performance of the Philharmonic orchestra in Plymouth. "I'm too pregnant to sit still," she complained. "My doctor says it's false labor, but it's the pits, nevertheless. Drew has gotten a movie, and we're staying home like old married people. Please take them; you'll love it."

"Are you sure, Holly? You've only got a couple of weeks till the real thing, and then you'll really be house-bound."

"Positive. Take them."

It would have been the perfect time to ask whether Ryan had tickets, but she didn't want to know, and more to the point, mentioning his name would incur an endless discussion of things she wasn't ready to rehash. If her friendship with Holly were to survive, it would have to do so in spite of Ryan. Sky had spent the past six days convincing herself that what was done was done. Insisting on more than what Ryan offered hadn't brought anything but misery. Misery, however, wasn't part of Jane Greenleaf Schuyler's nature. Come spring, the man would be out of her system. She just needed a few weeks—maybe months she conceded—to get her equilibrium back.

Kim agreed to go with Sky, and at seven-thirty Sky introduced herself to the Morella household in a small, neat house a mile past the police station, off Pilgrim Street. Kim's parents seemed relieved that their daughter was doing something that didn't include Eric. It seemed not so different from John and Sarah Schuyler's reaction that summer when Sky had spent a night with a girlfriend.

The only unpleasant surprise seemed to be a deliberate omission on Holly's part. The seats were part of a block: season's tickets for the Branigan family. The program included a full-page ad for Branigan Cranberries with a note that they underwrote a guest artist and were major corporate contributors. All six Branigans were listed, along with Anne and Holly, as sponsors or patrons.

Jody was already seated, without a date, and Kevin introduced her to his. As the lights dimmed, Ryan and Anne eased their way across the aisle. Ryan had the audacity to sit next to Sky, and her flesh rose into goose bumps from the nape of her neck to her fingertips. The baton was raised for the opening movement, but the pulse washing in her ears threatened to drown out every note.

Sky shifted, and the program fell off her lap. Ryan bent with her to retrieve it. "Hi," he whispered.

"Hello," she replied. She didn't say another word till intermission. When the houselights brightened, there was little choice. Ryan was cordial in his guarded, pensive way, as attentive to everyone else as he was to Sky. He made a point of asking Kim what she thought.

"Totally hot?" he joked.

"Not exactly," she replied.

As Ryan got up from his seat, he touched Sky's arm, and it was enough to make her jump. He gave her a look that told her he'd noticed, then helped Anne from their row and down the steps toward the refreshments. Kim went out to smoke, and Sky stayed alone in her seat. The teenager was the first to return.

Kim turned to Sky after fidgeting with her program. "Can I ask you something?" she whispered. "You know the guy you told me about? The one you thought knocked you up?"

"Kim!"

"You know what I mean. Was it Ryan?"

Sky looked at Kim's expectant expression but didn't reply.

"I've been thinking a lot about what you told me, Sky. He's got that way of looking at you, kind of outrageous and laid-back all at once. Eric says he's been a total pain in the—you know—*neck* all week, and you're real down, too."

"Ryan has a lot on his mind with his career, the rest is none of your business."

Kim just grinned and chewed the edge of her program. "I'll bet he was awesome when he was Eric's age. I'd be jacked, too, even now I guess, if he was hanging around all the time."

Sky sighed. "If he *were* hanging around, which he's not, and I'm not *jacked*, either! I just ran into him this winter after years and years."

"Well, you two look great together, you know. Everybody in here has been looking at you guys."

"We're not together," Sky replied, trying to remain calm. "He brought Sean's wife."

"Well, you should be."

The lights were blinking, much to Sky's relief. Her only regret was that the totally awesome cop was returning to his seat. "You should have come down for some cranberry juice," he whispered.

Sky flipped open her program. "Kim and I were talking."

Fifteen

Sky lay awake in bed. She'd taken to playing *what if* with herself. What if he hadn't lost his parents so young, would he be different? What if the Johanna thing hadn't been so hard on him? What if Peter Bancroft were still alive, and there was no pressure to bring him into the business full-time?

Would Ryan commit himself to a woman if he didn't have the security of his all-encompassing family? Was he a confirmed bachelor like Kevin, or more like Drew and Sean? Why did she care? Sky hated to answer that one.

She scoffed at herself and settled into the empty bed. She hadn't even asked him about the job or the chief or his brother's reactions. She wondered how long it would take for him to establish another relationship, then gave half a thought to taking things on his terms and pounded her pillow. The hell with him, she kept repeating. These first few weeks would be the toughest, then she'd go find herself a nice stockbroker dying to bare his soul to her.

At the end of their second week apart, the painters finished the first floor of Schuyler House. It was gleaming and fresh, and ready for her touch. She was ready for tropical drinks and the warmth of Palm Beach. The weather turned mean. The skies stayed gray, with snow promised daily. There was half a foot of it on the ground already, which Kevin insisted on plowing. He stayed for a cup of coffee and reported that the barn workshop was nearly finished, the bogs were flooded to protect against a hard freeze and Drew was restless and anxious over Holly. "She's as tough as the rest of us, just comes in a softer package. But Drew is a wreck 'cause their doctor is at Boston General. It may be the best care in the area, but it's a hike even in perfect conditions. It was Matt's suggestion, knowledgeable med student that he is."

"First babies take their time, anyway, don't they?" Sky asked.

"This one better," Kevin replied, and they both laughed.

"And Ryan?" she said finally.

Kevin looked at her as he got up from the table. "He put his name on the list. He deserves the position, and he'll probably get it. He's a very good cop."

Sky touched his arm. "I'm sorry things didn't work out the way you wanted."

Kevin nodded. "My fault in a way. He was sitting on his degree, and the job was a way to help with Matt's med-school tuition. I shoved him into it and then pushed too hard to get him out. He's as stubborn as I am, and I should have left him alone. It's all he wants now, but he's no good by himself. He just thinks he is." The double entendre was the only hint this reserved older brother gave Sky that he knew of the intensity of what passed as a relationship between his middle brother and the woman he'd had to drive home to her father one August night so many years before.

Sky had no intention of crying, but the tears welled up as she closed the door behind Kevin. She didn't want to have any feelings left for any of them until she was back on firm emotional ground, whenever that might be. The evening news predicted a full day of snow, and it was falling heavily before she'd finished dinner. Without the painters and the teenagers the big house seemed claustrophobic, as if she'd been locked in with nothing but her own restlessness.

She called her mother after dinner. It would have been safer to call Jake, but she thought of it too late. Her mother made the inevitable clucking sounds and insisted she come down for a respite from the weather. Holly's condition was a legitimate excuse. "I don't want to miss the arrival," Sky said, "and she's due in about a week." She hung up thinking of Ryan's admonition about her jumping ship the minute the weather didn't suit her. Maybe it was too late to change, and who cared, anyway, certainly not Ryan. Sky buttoned herself into a nightshirt and snuggled under the duvet to fight boredom, regret and the cold empty bed.

"You won't be imposing: *I* called *you*. I need some female company around here. With the storm, Drew wants us to get a hotel room in Boston or camp out at Matt's in case I go into labor. He's driving me crazy! Please say yes, and come over to stay. If we lose electricity, you don't want to be in that house all by yourself, anyway, Sky." Holly's happy pleading voice had woken Sky at nine the next morning. There was ten inches of fluff on the ground already, and Millbrook had come to a quiet standstill.

Sky sighed and smiled at the view from her window. "You don't want me there. Really, Holly, you and Drew should be together."

Holly laughed. "Don't romanticize this, Sky. I can barely go up and down the stairs, my EMT brothers-in-law keep taking my pulse and asking pointed questions, and Matt calls daily. He's doing a dermatology rotation at the same hospital, and boy, am I glad it's not obstetrics!"

Sky laughed, too. "Do they all have reasons to be nervous, Holly?"

Her friend hedged. "No, except that things do seem to be moving, the term is 'lightening' actually, but I'm anything *but* light! The baby is pressing and moving into position. Yesterday Dr. Barnes said I'll probably go within the week, but why he ever mentioned it to the future father is beyond me."

"Holly!"

"Not you, too. Now come on over. The weather bureau is saying three to five feet. We haven't had a blizzard since '78, and if I get snowed in with these four hovering males, I may never recover."

"Okay, okay, you win."

"Good. Sit tight, and Drew'll come for you in the pickup."

Sky packed a small bag with two things on her mind. Holly was more concerned than she let on, and Ryan would be impossible to avoid. Sky's determination to give her friend support overrode the discomfort she knew she'd feel. She dressed in faded jeans and an oversize fisherman-knit sweater, the Millbrook uniform. It was the same one she'd worn the afternoon Ryan pulled her from the bogs.

Drew arrived in the truck, with the plow in place, and gave the Schuyler driveway a good clearing even though the snow was still falling ominously. It had drifted into rippled patterns against her fence and danced in tiny tornadoes as she opened the mudroom door. "Andrew Branigan, are you sure you want me over there?"

"Please! Holly is torturing me with *Pagliacci* and *Madame Butterfly*, and opera is the one thing we can't agree on. They were Peter's records, and with my luck, this baby will arrive singing an aria. It's genetic with the Bancrofts." He sighed and shook the powder from his parka. "About every twenty minutes Holly rubs her back and sinks into a chair, moaning. I can't take much more."

There was concern written all over him, even though he laughed. Drew helped her into the truck's cab, and they made their way slowly out of the village. The snow covered everything, falling faster than the plows could scrape, and as a town plow passed, Drew shook his head. "They'll quit soon and wait till it settles some. We're in for it this time."

"It's beautiful, though," Sky said over the engine's noise. "I love the way it hangs in the pines." The landscape was hazy gray, and visibility had been reduced to fifty yards or less, zero when the squalls blew up. After three times the normal ten-minute run they reached the lane and headed down the path to the Bancroft side of the property. The neatly plowed outline of the parking area was blurred, and the path to the house obliterated. Kevin and Ryan's house wasn't even visible. Sky got out and turned her head toward the rumble and thunder of another truck.

"Ryan," Drew said. "He's plowing the barn. I don't care what he does down there as long as he keeps us open up here."

"You really are a wreck," Sky kidded as they worked their way to the porch.

Drew stopped before they climbed the steps. "Sky, Holly's got a will of iron. She put more energy into denying the truth about her discomfort than a man puts into harvesting. I know her—hell, I love her for it most of the time—but she's uncomfortable, and I have the feeling that she's in there willing this baby to slow down. Damn it, I'd give anything to have some idea of what she's feeling."

"First babies can take forever; that much I know," Sky replied hopefully.

"That's about how much time we'll need if anything happens," Drew said.

They reached the door, and Drew opened it to the blast of an operatic finale. "Ah," Sky said, "The count is forgiving Susanna, *The Marriage of Figaro*."

Drew looked at her sideways. "Not you, too."

"You *do* remember the summer I got shipped off to Austria? What's Vienna without Mozart!"

Holly waddled from the kitchen, with a spoon in hand, and a man-size apron tied under her breasts. "Even more reason to have you wait out the storm with us! And in your honor, I decided to throw together Peter's recipe for chowder. It's a Bancroft tradition, apparently. He used to fix it and serve it up when these guys were up all night monitoring the bogs during the frost warnings or plowing. Ryan refused to let me marry into the family until I'd perfected it."

Drew, who had taken Sky's bag upstairs to her room, clomped back down in his knee-high boots. "I'll be shoveling down the hill. Use the pager if you need me, sweetheart." He kissed her and sighed. "I love you."

"I know," Holly replied. "Go keep yourself busy and tell the rest that soup's on at four-thirty." Her hair was piled on top of her head, and her complexion glowed. She was the picture of happiness.

When Drew had gone out, Holly turned to Sky. "I was afraid if I told you everybody was coming for supper, you might not join us."

"Because of Ryan?"

"You're not exactly making a beeline to the barn anymore."

Sky sighed. "I suppose it's not his fault. He's a realist, and my life-style only appeals from a distance. He'd be back in a minute if I agreed to his terms, I think."

"Which are?"

"A nice affair completely removed from the rest of his life. He wants me in some distant corner, but always available."

Holly was absentmindedly rubbing her lower back. "Symptomatic, if you ask me, and I know you haven't, of feelings too deep to think about."

"Right!"

"I might be, you never know. Ryan's in the middle. He's got the drive and the strength of them all put together, but he hasn't got the goal. Nobody's drifted but Ryan, and it makes him different. He thinks he wants to be a cop; I think he wants to save the world, at least the part that's under twenty. He dotes on Katey and Suzanne—the paternal instinct needing a place to light." Holly barely stopped for a breath.

"He's the closest thing I've got to a brother, but he lets me in because I'm married to Drew and no risk. To quote my adorable husband on the subject, you knocked Ryan's socks off, and he'd rather eat nails than admit it. Find out why, if it's important to you. I know damn well it is."

"So Cupid wears maternity clothes," Sky remarked quietly.

Holly patted Sky's arm. "Hit him with both barrels as soon as it's appropriate." She moved again to rub the small of her back.

"While we're being so honest with each other, how are you feeling, *really*?"

"Like the baby's done a swan dive and landed face-down, ready to get this show on the road. No contractions, just crampy and achy."

"And Dr. Barnes knows?"

"Certainly. He's says I'm right on schedule, probably within the week. The snow wasn't forecast to bury us when I was in his office. First babies take hours, and once the storm stops, the roads'll be plowed, and all these overgrown baby-sitters can relax. The only one who is staying calm is Anne."

At four o'clock the sound of thumping on the porch made Sky look up from the salad she was making. Snow-covered men, each as handsome and bundled up as the next, knocked snow from their boots and blew on their hands as they pulled off gloves. Holly snapped on the outside light, which further illuminated Kevin, Drew and Ryan.

"I'll build a fire," Sky said suddenly and wandered into the living room where logs already lay on the andirons. She was fumbling with kindling when Ryan knelt next to her, with Katey Branigan clinging to his neck.

"Need a match?"

Sky pivoted from her squatting position. "Thanks." It was worse than the tug she'd felt when she thought he was married. It was worse than a blind date. It was awful. Ryan didn't seem to notice.

"Down you go, pumpkin," he murmured to his niece, who scooted back to the kitchen. "Sky, may I talk to you a minute?"

"That would be a pleasant change," she said, surprising herself with the sarcasm.

He put his hand over hers and although she could feel his stare, she looked on as the logs ignited. "Listen for a minute," he said. "If Holly goes into labor in the next two days, there's not a snowball's chance that we can get her to the hospital unless we decide that even the smallest cramps are the beginning of labor. They've closed Route 3 completely until the storm stops. Plymouth General is a possibility, but her doctor is in Boston."

Sky's expression matched Ryan's. "But she's not due till next week."

"You're right, and all this will probably blow over, but she's dilating, and she's got low back pain. Watch her yourself, Sky. She's hiding the discomfort."

"Ryan!"

"Drew and I talked to Barnes from the house a while ago. Sean's just come off his shift, and I'm off unless I get an emergency call. We're both EMTs, and we've both handled emergency deliveries, not to mention Sean's own kids."

"You can't possibly be suggesting—"

"Sky, I'm just covering all the bases, and the obstetrician agrees it would be safer to deliver here and then travel. All I'm asking is that *if* she goes into labor, you'll promise to support us and not take her side if she gets panicky."

Sky put her face in her hands. "I don't know anything about this!"

"Exactly. The storm is no joke, and she's far safer here. Drew agrees. They've been to childbirth classes, they're prepared and everything's normal, no complications."

"No complications! Ryan this could be disastrous. Anything could happen here. I'd never be able to convince her," Sky gasped.

He grabbed her by the shoulders. "Janey Schuyler, for once in your life do what you're told! I love Holly as much as if she were my own sister. She's brought this family together. I don't like this any more than you do, and I know she'll hit the roof if I suggest it but, by God, I'm gonna keep her safe. I'm prepared for the worst; it's the way my mind works," he finished sullenly.

"And her doctor agrees?"

"Under these conditions, yes."

"Oh, God," she sighed as Drew called them from the doorway of the dining room.

"Soup's on," he said with forced brightness.

A buffet had been set up, and they took their chowder and salad to the fire and the television. Helicopter photos of stranded commuters and police chiefs' eyewitness accounts of rescues made Sky's spine tingle. They all sat glued to the set, including the girls who thought it all a wonderful game. Holly was biting her lip and eating very little. Sky caught her taking deep, then shallow breaths twice.

Ryan kept his distance, and when Holly got up to clear her place, Ryan followed with his arm around her shoulder. She was shaking her head vehemently as they went into the kitchen. The pain of being cut off from this side of Ryan dug at Sky as much as her fear for Holly.

Sky poked at the fire and found Drew next to her. "Nervous?" she asked.

"This is unbelievable. Ryan's giving you pep talks, and now Holly. It's a foregone conclusion as far as he and Sean are concerned. We should have driven into Matt's when the snow started."

"Drew, nobody knew it wasn't going to stop. My goodness, you Branigans run your whole livelihood around the quirks of the weather. You must know better than anyone how wrong a forecast can be."

"Cheery thought," he mumbled.

Anne and Sean gathered up their girls at six with lots of sincere advice about not worrying, and Kevin walked down the hill shortly thereafter. When Ryan was ready to go, Drew, Holly and Sky stood at the front door with him and watched the snow fall straight and silent. The wind had stopped. As Ryan turned to leave, he put his hands on Holly's cheeks. "Tomorrow when we wake up, the sun will be out and the plows will be moving. You can have all the contractions you want."

"Go home," Holly muttered.

He grinned and gave Sky what she took to be a meaningful look. "Ah, she's got days to go. See you guys in the morning" were his final words before he stepped from the lamplight into the stormy darkness.

Sky stayed up with her hosts until ten, watching TV, though the programs were constantly interrupted by weather updates. When the announcement came on that Plymouth and part of Duxbury had lost power, Sky's heart fell. So much for the local hospital as an alternative to the impossible trip to Boston.

Sky was in bed and nearly asleep by ten-thirty after assurances from Holly that though she felt crampy there were no contractions. Sky sighed, wrapped in a cocoon of expectation that bordered on fear for the circumstances. She didn't want to dwell on what might happen, but it was better than thinking about Ryan and the disintegration of what had passed as their relationship. The more she saw him interacting with his family, the more obvious it was to her how minor her role had been.

It seemed that Ryan was there with her, but it was a dream, shaken from her as a voice whispered her name. She bolted into a sitting position as Drew's hands found her shoulders. "Sky," he repeated, "are you awake?"

"Drew, yes, of course!"

His voice was barely audible, and Sky's hand was already at her heart. "Holly's in the bathroom; her water broke. Go downstairs so she doesn't hear you and call Sean or Ryan. There are still no contractions—tell either one of them. Can you do that for me quietly?"

"Yes," she said again, forcing cheerfulness. *For once in your life, do what you're told* came ringing back into her head. It was never too late to start.

Sixteen

Sky moved through the deep gray shadows of the first floor, oblivious to the voices above her. Her heart thundered, and she never felt the cold night air against her bare legs. She hit her hip on the corner of the dining room table but didn't turn on a light until she got to the kitchen. She squinted in the brightness and tapped out the only Branigan number she knew by heart. It was answered on the second ring.

"Kevin? Ryan?"

"Ryan," he replied, fully alert.

"Nobody needs you yet," she whispered, which wasn't completely true, "but Drew wanted you to know that Holly's water broke. She's not having contractions, though."

He swore under his breath, which didn't do much for Sky's confidence.

"Ryan, I'm scared," Sky blurted out before she had time to think.

He paused. "Don't be. Nothing's happening yet, and if it does, the last thing she needs is you falling apart."

He must have realized that his tone stung as much as his words. "Come on, Foxy," he added. "You've always been one for adventure. This may be the best one yet. Now hang up. Tell Drew I'm calling Dr. Barnes, and then I'll be over."

"They said they didn't need anyone," she replied.

"What do they know," he added. "They've never had a baby."

Sky snapped on the porch light and a lamp in the living room. It was three o'clock in the morning. She unlocked the door and went back upstairs, knocking lightly when she saw the sliver of light at Drew and Holly's threshold.

"Come in," Holly said. She was sitting up, her eyes glistening. "I guess Drew told you?"

"I had her call my brothers," Drew broke in, "and they'll call Barnes."

Holly simply nodded. The next sound was footsteps taking the stairs two at a time, and Sky turned just as Ryan appeared at the bedroom door in his socks, jeans, and a warm confident expression. "Holly Bancroft Branigan, you've been nothing but trouble since the night you tried to burn this house down."

He looked once at Sky's nightshirt before he moved to the edge of the bed. Holly laughed, but her eyes brimmed with tears that spilled over. Drew was beside her instantly. "Come on, city mouse, we're in this together."

Holly sniffed. "Get me out of here, Drew, while I'm still not in labor. I've never asked anything of you in my whole life. I don't care if Plymouth General is lit by candles: it's a hospital, damn it. First babies take days, remember?''

Ryan took her hand. ''Plymouth General is on generators, but it's chaos over there. And Holly, love, I'm not sure we could even get you down the lane to the road, let alone through these country streets. Nothing's moving and that includes you. I talked with your obstetrician, and the Millbrook Fire Department, and they both want you here.''

As if she had something to prove, Holly got herself into a sitting position, slid her feet to the floor and stood up. Her flannel gown billowed over her distended stomach, and she patted it. ''Then we'll just sit and wait, till this foolishness is over, and I can do this like a proper twentieth-century woman.'' She wiped the tears away.

''When has a Branigan ever waited for anything?'' Ryan said. ''I've got everything we need downstairs.''

''Don't you come near me with any of it!''

Drew looked at Ryan. ''Nasty already. Do we think she's in transition?'' A lot less playfully, he eased her back on the bed. ''As long as you're feeling so fabulous, try and go back to sleep. Rest at least, darling, please.''

''Drew is right,'' Sky added, feeling useless. ''Rest. I'll be in the next room if you need me.'' She was the first to leave them, knowing she was the last one anybody would call if the crisis arose. Sky dozed fitfully and gave up the idea of sleep altogether less than forty-five minutes later. She pulled her jeans back on and went downstairs, noting that Drew and Holly's threshold was dark.

Ryan was lying on the couch with an arm slung over his eyes, one socked foot sticking off the end and the other balanced on the coffee table. A light was on in the bedroom, and she found Sean stripping the mattress. ''Hi,'' he whispered. ''Anne's awfully glad you're over here.''

He smoothed what looked to be shower curtain liners under an old sheet and plumped some pillows. "This was Peter's grandparents' bed and his father was born in it. I don't suppose that'll cheer Holly any; but it's kind of nice to think about, though."

"You really expect it all to happen here, don't you?" Sky asked.

Sean nodded. "There's a good chance she's already started contractions. We would have given the ride a shot in the morning, but with the snow coming down and without daylight, there's no way." The sound of footsteps on the stairs interrupted them, and when Sky stepped into the foyer, she found Drew and Holly on the stairs. Ryan was already on his feet.

Drew looked at Ryan and said, "Ten minutes apart, twice."

Holly looked at Sky. "I'm glad I talked you into coming over here."

"Is there anything I can do, boil water or anything?"

"Yes, put on *Rigoletto*," Holly quipped.

"Come on, love," Drew complained.

"Humor me, I'm in pain," Holly snapped. The two of them made their way to the spare bedroom. "Branigans! I should have sold this when I had the chance."

Sky busied herself with the stereo and the coffee maker, marveling at Ryan's calm professionalism and fighting the knot of tension and apprehension in herself. It was still mixed with affection for all of them. Let me in, she wanted to cry.

Sky ventured back to the bedroom and found Sean on the phone with the obstetrician, Ryan standing and Drew breathing with Holly as she got through a contraction. Ryan had removed a pair of surgical gloves and pulled another sterile pair from the medical supply kit at the foot of the bed.

"Jump box," he said to Sky as she looked at it. "Each squad car and the ambulance are equipped with them. Let's get a cup of coffee and give these guys some privacy."

Sky poured mugs for Sean and Ryan and then herself. "I suppose everything is happening the way it's supposed to?"

"I'm no expert, but from what I've been taught, everything is perfect. She's dilating rapidly, probably has been for the past two days. Once she gets to about three minutes apart, it'll be quick." Ryan gave Sean a grateful look. "I'm glad you're here."

Sean laughed. "Katey arrived in thirty-five minutes, bless her heart. I know Holly's frightened and probably embarrassed, but once transition hits, she won't think about anything but that little kiddo." He looked out into the still-dark night. "This sure beats the side of the road or the back of my ambulance."

As *Rigoletto* finished, the sky had begun to lighten. Outside a truck rumbled, and Sky caught sight of Kevin working the plow. The snow was reduced to flurries that danced in his headlights as he inched his way up the lane to the house. Even to Sky's restricted view she could see that the going was slow and treacherous. She fiddled with background music and built a fire as dawn inched its way over the white, bedazzled landscape.

She listened but offered little as Sean and Ryan talked, and after another hour, the fire fighter called the ambulance crew from the kitchen phone and told them they'd be needed before noon.

While Sky poked a log, Ryan came up to her as he had the night before. He stared at the flames, his face tight, his body tense.

"You're wonderful with Holly," Sky said softly.

Ryan's expression didn't change. "Drew waited a long time for her. I can't let anything happen."

"Are you scared?" she asked, and he finally turned to face her.

"I'd be a fool not to be."

"She's very lucky to have you care that much, Ryan," Sky said, trying to continue, but her throat tightened and she turned away.

Drew called his brothers at that moment, and she was left alone at the fire. Sean was back quickly. "Sky would you crush some ice and put it in a facecloth? Holly wants you; she says she's tired of Irish madmen. This is transition. I'm gonna call Barnes again; we're on our way."

As quickly as she could, Sky rapped ice into chips, found a clean linen dish cloth and hurried back through the house. Kevin had reached the top of the hill, and she watched the red taillights flash as he pushed the two days' offering aside, inching his way out to the road with the pickup truck.

Holly was propped in her antique Bancroft bed, with Drew kneeling behind her as she leaned into a contraction. Sean was in the corner of the room on the phone with the doctor, relaying the progress. Ryan was sitting on the edge of the mattress. He took the ice from Sky and waited.

"Shallow," Drew demanded until Holly panted and collapsed back against him, and Ryan handed her the cloth.

Sky found herself panting, too, her heart racing with the tension. Holly's efforts were valiant and precise, the result of classes and Drew's coaching. Every time she cried out, shivers shot up Sky's back, but Drew never missed a beat in his encouragement. Ryan clenched his jaw. "Sky?"

"I'm right here," she whispered behind him.

"Sterile diapers and a bath towel—"

She was on the stairs immediately. She washed her hands first because it seemed appropriate, then got the items from the nursery. It was seven-twenty by the Mickey Mouse clock.

Oaths she hadn't heard since she'd been a teenager shot out of the first-floor bedroom as she came back downstairs. "I can't damn it, I can't!" Holly's voice was cut off by a gasp that sent fear spinning through Sky. She hurried in with the diapers. Drew was the only one who looked as though he might believe his wife, but he was still telling her that she most certainly could.

Sean said "She's crowning" into the receiver and motioned to Ryan to move his hands. "Keep her going."

Sky pressed back against the dresser and held her breath, her eyes riveted on Ryan as he leaned forward.

"One for Drew, Holly," he said, "Now!"

Holly sat up and put every last drop of strength into the effort.

Sky's view was obscured as Ryan leaned down and shifted his gloved hands. "One more for the rest of us, love." Holly complied. With a hushed *pop* a perfect baby girl slithered into her uncle's hands.

"Maria!" Drew cried as Ryan wiped the tiny mouth. She was already howling.

"Maria Bancroft Branigan," Holly said and then buried her face in Drew's shoulder, sobbing, laughing, oblivious to Ryan's hand, which firmly massaged the plane of muscle between her navel and pubic bone. He stopped long enough to reach for a diaper and vigorously rub the baby, then put her at Holly's breast. In a few moments the placenta was delivered, and Maria was wrapped snugly next to her mother. Drew got knee socks on Holly's feet, kissed her soundly and wiped his eyes. Chaos reigned. Sean hung up, called the ambulance from his portable and went in search of his oldest brother.

Within the next fifteen minutes, mother, baby, placenta, blankets and Drew were bundled into the pickup truck for the trip down the lane to the waiting ambulance. Sean climbed into the back, and shafts of sunlight broke through the dispersing clouds.

Sky turned from the window in the suddenly still house and went back into the bedroom to remove the linens. She stared at the bed for a long time and then put the towels in a bundle and the plastic in the bathtub. With the bundle in her arms, Sky went into the laundry area. Ryan was at the sink with his face buried in his hands. As she cleared her throat, he moved suddenly and splashed handfuls of water over his face. Sky focused on the perfect snowflakes pressed on Holly's kitchen window.

"You were magnificent," she whispered.

"Nature's magnificent," he replied with a catch in his voice. He balled his fist against the furrow on his forehead, as if willing composure. The tension had drained from him, and in these mellow moments, Sky's apprehension returned.

I'm losing him, she thought, *he's pulling away completely.* "Will you be called out this afternoon for police work to help with the snow emergency?" she asked in a painfully impersonal voice.

"No, I took my name off the list yesterday."

Sky dropped her bundle on the lid of the washing machine. "You mean you resigned?"

"In a way, yes. It's over."

Something in her snapped. "You didn't tell me! My God, Ryan, we've just spent hours together, most of them killing time, and you never thought to mention your decision?" Her own hand went to her eyes. Unwanted tears stung, and she wiped them away furiously. "What's the use. I'm sorry. I hope your brothers didn't pressure you into it; I know it was your first love."

Fatigue hung on his shoulders, and he looked at her for a long time before he turned to the coffee maker. "*You* were my first love," he said abruptly. Both his hands shook as he poured the liquid, and it sloshed from the mug onto his knuckles.

"Ryan!" Without asking, she ran the cold tap and pushed his hands under, then dabbed them with a dish towel. Over the terry cloth they finally looked at each other, green eyes, blue eyes, pools of emotion. "I was hardly the first," she continued. "Maybe just the one who held out the longest."

He shook his head slowly and put down the towel. "You were the first one, Sky. I just tried like hell not to let you know. It was damned important then to be better at something than you and better than the competition."

"You didn't have any," she whispered. "I always thought I was just another—"

"You never told me about thinking you were pregnant. I never knew. It's all I've thought about since you threw the news at me."

The morning air was charged with the night's tension. They both felt raw with it. Sky watched Ryan and knew as well as she'd ever known anything, that these moments would change their lives. Whether for better or worse, she couldn't fathom.

"Ryan, you're right, you know. I've had just about everything I ever wanted, and that includes you. I wanted you so badly I was willing to play everything on your terms, but it's over. It's a cheap excuse for real life, and it makes me feel cheated. It all fell together for me tonight. I've been watching your real life as if I were the wallpaper. Your skill and your tenderness, the family business and babies, and pressure from those who love you and the way you love them back. That's what hurts the most.

"It's like a steel rod that keeps you straight. It made Holly trust you with her life. Those boys trust you the way they've never trusted an authority figure before. You cheated me out of all of it. I love your family; I love Holly," she said with a sigh, and the tears welled up again. "I love you, Ryan. I've always loved you, and the hell of it is I thought you could love me back, but you can't, and the role of just another woman in your life isn't for me. At least I can thank you for letting me see that much."

Ryan stood absolutely still. "'Just another woman' doesn't even begin to scratch the surface. You ruined me for any other woman: there's no one else in the world like you, Sky, and I've looked. A long time ago you made me restless, and you made me look at myself. You were a dream I held—one that came true and then vanished. Why would I want to go through that again? This time around I gave you everything it was safe to give."

"I know, Ryan. That much I know."

Ryan turned to the window and watched the clouds drift past the sun. "I meant what I said in Boston. If Millbrook doesn't suit you, you'll be gone with the next wind, but this is where I belong. I took a long time coming home. It's not always wonderful but I want to work with my brothers. This is what I want." He looked at her and held the glance. "Please don't cry: it tears me apart. I don't want any more tears and regrets and mistakes."

"Mistakes!" Her blue eyes flashed. "I've made more mistakes than you getting to this point. There's nowhere else I'd go because I'm tired of running away from my feelings. It doesn't work. I'm sorry I'm rich. I'm sorry I have family in Florida, but that's who I am.

"Branigan, I love Millbrook. I love Schuyler House. I love Kim, and she needs me even if you don't. I would never betray that trust. You're just going to have to move over because I'm not giving up my home and my friends just because you and I can't make things work."

Sky crossed the room. "Millbrook had better be big enough for both of us, because I'll be damned if some lamebrained hunk of a cranberry grower makes me so miserable I even consider giving it all up! The Schuylers were here generations before the Branigans, and we'll be here generations after. And while we're on the subject, I'm *not* shallow and flighty; I'm just scared to death of losing you."

The tears were gone, and the room was so bright that dust motes sparkled in the shafts of sunlight. She pointed a finger at him. "You're the only thing I couldn't have, and the one thing I need most. We're not two virgins sneaking out to the golf course. We're adults with adult problems and adult feelings. I love you Ryan Branigan; it's not simple but there it is."

Sky stopped long enough to glare at him, and her look softened as she read his face. "You told me you were scared a while ago, but you weren't. You just wanted to be careful, to make everything perfect for Drew and Holly. Well, you can't be careful when you love somebody the way I love you. You'll never know what love really feels like till you jump in with both feet. Trust me, Ryan, the way Holly trusted you. Trust me with everything that you are. Give me what you give to your family. You'll never be sorry. I dare you.''

"I love you," he sighed, as if it were the most painful confession in the world. "It's the surest thing I know and the hardest thing to say."

She smiled. "Practice it, then."

"I love you. Nothing in my life ever felt so right and scared me so much."

"That's quite a confession coming from a former police officer and juvenile delinquent." Sky touched his beard-roughened face.

"Well, it's the truth. I can't change overnight. I've been fighting this a long time, Sky, fighting myself as much as you."

They were walking through the empty house, and they paused at the foyer, with the stairs on the left and the bedroom just ahead. "Magnificent," Sky whispered. "You made everything perfect. If we start right this minute, a little at a time, we can make life perfect for each other. Not overnight..."

"I'm not an easy person, and this isn't an easy life," Ryan said.

"Perfect doesn't have to be easy."

Meanwhile, the Millbrook ambulance made its slow, careful way to the emergency room of the closest hospital. Maria Bancroft Branigan, born in her grandfather's bed, named for her grandmother, lay bundled at her mother's breast, cuddled by her father. Sean Branigan saw them safely off and went home, still teary-eyed, to breakfast with his family. Kevin continued to plow out the property and made a mental note to check the

Schuyler House driveway when the village streets were passable.

Over the sounds of the distant plows, Sky whispered, "Talk to me, Ryan."

They went upstairs, and in the long tender moments that followed, "I love you" were the only words he spoke and the only ones she needed to hear.

Look for *Something in Common* (#376) by Leslie Davis Guccione, Kevin Branigan's story, coming in September 1987 from Silhouette Desires.

READERS' COMMENTS ON SILHOUETTE DESIRES

"Thank you for Silhouette Desires. They are the best thing that has happened to the bookshelves in a long time."

—V.W.*, Knoxville, TN

"Silhouette Desires—wonderful, fantastic—the best romance around."

—H.T.*, Margate, N.J.

"As a writer as well as a reader of romantic fiction, I found DESIREs most refreshingly realistic—and definitely as magical as the love captured on their pages."

—C.M.*, Silver Lake, N.Y.

"I just wanted to let you know how very much I enjoy your Silhouette Desire books. I read other romances, and I must say your books rate up at the top of the list."

—C.N.*, Anaheim, CA

"Desires are number one. I especially enjoy the endings because they just don't leave you with a kiss or embrace; they finish the story. Thank you for giving me such reading pleasure."

—M.S.*, Sandford, FL

*names available on request